Drawing Nudes While Making Other Plans

Drawing Nudes While Making Other Plans

Zoe Gaetjens

PENGUIN BOOKS

PENGUIN BOOKS

UK | USA | Canada | Ireland | Australia
India | New Zealand | South Africa | China

Penguin Random House Australia

Penguin Random House Australia is part of the Penguin Random House group of companies whose addresses can be found at global.penguinrandomhouse.com.

First published by Penguin, an imprint of Penguin Random House Australia Pty Ltd, in 2026

Cover design by Hazel Lam
Cover image: Mari Dein/stock.adobe.com
Typeset in 11.5/16.5 pt Goudy Old Style by Midland Typesetters, Australia

Printed and bound in Australia by Griffin Press, an accredited ISO AS/NZS 14001 Environmental Management Systems printer

NATIONAL LIBRARY OF AUSTRALIA

A catalogue record for this book is available from the National Library of Australia

FSC www.fsc.org MIX Paper | Supporting responsible forestry FSC® C018684

ISBN 978 1 76135 801 2 (Paperback)

We at Penguin Random House Australia acknowledge that Aboriginal and Torres Strait Islander peoples are the Traditional Custodians and the first storytellers of the lands on which we live and work. We honour Aboriginal and Torres Strait Islander peoples' continuous connection to Country, waters, skies and communities. We celebrate Aboriginal and Torres Strait Islander stories, traditions and living cultures; and we pay our respects to Elders past and present.

To Paul, who finally read my book.

Plan for your Final Year of School

By Emmaline Markson, for Cleo Markson

I've started year 12 and here's what I've learnt so far. You won't need this plan right away, but I hope it will help when you get there.

1. *Choose subjects you like, bonus points if you are good at them.*
2. *Listen in class. This feels a little obvious, but you'd be surprised at the number of classmates I've seen disappointed with results when they've literally paid no attention.*
3. *Study. It's a boring one, but important. Depending on where I end up, I'll help if I can, except for art, obviously. Unless you want suggestions on the best ways to draw stick figures or worms. I reckon I'm pretty good at both.*
4. *Keep your life in balance. I've made comments about the school stuff, but you have to balance it out with everything else. So, with that in mind:*

a) Continue swimming.

b) Get a job and start saving.

c) Start to build your social life!!!

5. *To help with 4c: find your friends. Your real ones.*
6. *In your free time, try some new things. My suggestions are as follows:*
   - *Explore Sydney a little more.*
   - *Go to a party, if you haven't done that already. (I know it's not your usual scene, but it's a rite of passage – and remember 4c!)*
   - *First kiss?! Who knows, maybe by the time you hit year 12 this will already have already happened? (I hope so, but if not, here is my quick pep talk . . . You said you can't comprehend anyone liking you enough to stick their tongue down your throat – your words, not mine – but maybe you need to be ready? Despite what you think, you ARE very likeable!! And so is kissing. For more details see my very useful 'Plan for First Kisses'.)*
7. *Work out what you want to do when you finish year 12.*

You got this, Cleo! It's going to be great.

Chapter One

I am not late. I am absolutely not late. I can feel the heat rising in my cheeks and my heart beating at an unnaturally fast pace and I want to tell the fifty people who are turning to look at me that I was fifteen minutes *early* for the bus. That I planned it all out. That it wasn't my fault the bus came late, which meant I missed the early train, which meant that the time buffer I set up for things like finding the correct entrance to the Art School was no longer in play. I want to tell them that as thankful as I am for GPS – and believe me, I am overwhelmingly thankful – I still got lost walking from the back entrance to the gallery space where the induction had already begun.

Well, maybe I don't want to tell them that bit.

The fact is, I made it. I travelled to the Australian Art School. By myself. So, even though my face feels hot to touch, and my heart is racing, and I have unnaturally sweaty pits, I *am* proud of myself. But can I tell any of that to the fifty-odd students gathered in this sandstone building? No. No, I cannot. To them I am late and already out of place.

I try not to wish Emmaline was with me. My sister would have wrapped her arm around me and won everyone over with her massive smile and a big wave. But she is not here.

By the door is what looks to be an abandoned welcome table. It holds a single information folder. Mine. A sticky label reading *Cleo Markson* has been placed just under the Australian Art School logo.

I have clearly missed the introduction of the woman up the front. But her slides tell me her name is Rachael Ramirez and I am pretty sure my letter of invitation was signed by her. Further confirmation I am in the right spot. Not that I need it, but I'm pleased to have remembered the program organiser's name. I grab my info pack and attempt to scout out a place to sit.

Before becoming home to the Art School, the sandstone buildings here used to house prisoners. According to my research, aka last night's stress googling, the building that serves as the gallery/meeting point/induction space is the old prison chapel. I'm surprised that, despite its repurposing, the gallery is still filled with old church pews.

Let me tell you, a pew is not the latecomer's best friend. Don't get me wrong, pews are almost works of art themselves, but everyone probably arrived on time in prison chapel days and I'm sure they filed in in a very orderly manner and no one had to worry themselves about things like where to sit. Sure, life would have been tough, but working out the optimal seating plan was probably not up there in the list of troubles.

My choice of seats is limited. There looks to be a spacious spot up front, but there is no way on God's green earth I am about to make my way up there, so I scoot into the nearest opening I can find.

It's not until I sit that I realise my chosen spot is not really a spot at all. It's more like . . . *half* of a spot. And yet I can't bear to get up and draw attention to myself again.

I perch on the edge of the seat and cross my legs. Maybe balancing on one arse cheek will take up less room.

I try to concentrate on Rachael Ramirez's welcome speech.

'We are so very proud to provide this opportunity, not just to students from our Sydney schools but also to those from further afield. The human body is to be celebrated. In its variety, it is a thing of beauty. Out there, our differences may separate us, but here we believe that the body should be what unites us, what connects us.' At this she raises her arms, slotting her fingers together so her hands are now linked. A physical demonstration of what she is talking about. 'During this summer workshop we will focus on the naked form, using it as inspiration to create art, to build skills, to learn new techniques, to experiment and to create lasting connections. We are stripping back and building up, carving, sculpting, sketching and finding the truth that's buried beneath.'

I manage to stifle my snort with a little cough. I've obviously been at a public school too long. *Get it together, Cleo. You are not a thirteen-year-old boy*, I tell myself sternly. *If you can't hear the word naked or stripping without laughing, you're certainly not going to be able to make it through four weeks of drawing nudes.*

My one-butt-cheek seat perch is a mistake. I can't maintain it. It's not a comfortable position and I figure I'm already crowding my neighbour, so I give in and slide back on the pew so I can rest against it. My back is hunched into a u shape and my shoulders are now squished against my neighbour's. My thigh is pressed against his and I am all too aware that this proximity with a stranger is not normally socially acceptable.

I try to focus on Rachael, but the heat slowly building in my thigh is absolutely distracting. In these close quarters, turning my head to offer my neighbour an apology half smile feels like an invasion of privacy. I can't see his face, but I can see his legs. He's wearing loose-fitting dark grey pants and I can see a glimpse of olive skin above his white Nike kicks. Out of the corner of my eye I can just make out a slightly oversized white tee with a Thrills logo to the left. He has a chunky brown watchband on his left wrist and muscular forearms. His welcome packet sits on his lap. His name might be Matt? I can only see the start of it. Matthew? Matteo? Mattholemew? No, that's not even a real name. I don't think.

Oh my gosh. Focus!

I force my attention back to the front. I am determined this workshop will be a good way to spend my Christmas holidays. My art teacher selected me out of our year 11 visual art class.

'This is a wonderful opportunity for you, Cleo,' she said. 'You will learn so much, really develop as an artist. This will increase your confidence too. I think this could guide your major work.'

I found out later that I wasn't Miss Saidi's first choice. I wasn't surprised. I probably would have picked Yasmin Lin first too. She is topping the class. If anyone can get a Band 6 in visual arts it's her, but funnily enough she doesn't even care; she just creates for the joy of it. It's like she enters this zone when she paints, headphones in, only focused on what's in front of her. So confident in the choices she is making. I always feel jealous when I see her in this kind of flow. It's not necessarily her skill I want but the degree of certainty with which she holds her brush and makes her mark. Like she knows what she wants and will just go for it. Unlike me. I second-guess every stroke. *Is this right? Does it look good? Will this shade work?* I'm overly self-conscious. Utterly indecisive. In art and in life. So, while Yasmin would have thrived here, the best I can hope for from the program is direction. Whatever. I am certainly in need of direction. And something different to do over these remaining four weeks of summer holidays, as my parents keep reminding me.

Once Rachael Ramirez finishes her speech, we are invited to exit the gallery/meeting point/induction space/old prison chapel for a morning tea served outside. I reach down to grab my bag and take a moment to shove my welcome pack in. I've got a long trip home and the reading material will be a great distraction.

I turn to speak to Matt/Matthew/Matteo. I want to apologise for squishing in next to him. It will be good to meet someone, seeing as I literally know no one here.

'Hey. I'm sorry for the squishy intro –' I start to say to Matt/Matthew/Matteo standing and turning finally to face him. But all I see is his back. He has unfolded himself from his place next to me and is making his way to the door.

Thanks so much for giving me a second of your time to introduce yourself before running away.

I'm not sure why I'm so bugged by the fact that he has just left me hanging after our weirdly intimate pew moment. But I feel irrationally bothered. Mum would tell me to move on. That it's not all about me, that I just need to brush it off, like it feels he did to me. Water off a duck's back and all that. It's not that it's bad advice but give me a minute to apologise. We may have shared a very uncomfortable fifteen minutes, but it's not like I have leprosy.

I make the important decision not to chase Matt/Matthew/Matteo like some loser desperate for someone to talk to, and follow the group outside. Bag over my shoulder, I head towards the morning tea table while some of the other students start to chat. I focus on my food selection so I won't have to work out who to have an awkward conversation with.

It's an impressive spread. My stomach grumbles and I am reminded that it was dark out when I last ate. I select an apple Danish and a caramel slice and place them on top of a serviette in my hand. I shuffle through the other students to the tea and coffee table.

'Urgh, International Roast,' a girl grumbles. 'Are they trying to poison us on our first day? Hard pass.' She puts her cup back down.

I take a very non-recyclable cup and reach for the tea bags. 'It's times like these I'm glad I don't drink coffee,'

I say, thankful that someone has chosen to talk to me, or at least talk in the vicinity of me.

'What? No coffee?' she asks.

'No, not really.'

'Not even when it's been a late night, and you've been up putting the finishing touches on your photographic essay and then your baby brother wakes you at 5.30 am because he wants to play?'

'That sounds weirdly specific, but still no.' *Also, thank you for talking to me so I don't have to work out who to talk to.* I don't say the last bit out loud.

'What if it was a really great flat white?'

'Nope.'

'A latte? Skinny cap? Long black? Macchiato?'

I am not a coffee person. These sound like something between made-up words and racial profiles. I don't say this out loud either. 'I don't know what they are. Are you making up words, or are we still talking about coffee? I really don't like coffee,' I say.

She laughs.

'I don't understand it, but fair enough. I'm Remi.'

Do we shake hands in this situation? I'm not sure. My hands are too full.

I mime shaking her hand with my refreshment pile. 'I'm Cleo.'

'Nice to meet you, Cleo.'

I focus on Remi. Her black hair is clipped in a short funky bob and blue eyeliner artfully adorns the crinkled corners of her eyes.

'So, what's your go-to coffee order?' I ask.

'The classic flat white for sure. I'll never say no to a flat white. But if you asked my mum, she would say I'm a latte,' Remi says. I must look like I don't get it. 'Like, I'm a lot, aye? A latte? Sorry, terrible joke. That's what happens when I'm forced to operate without sufficient refreshment.'

I laugh. If we hadn't had this interaction, I'm not sure I would have worked up the nerve to talk to Remi. She gives off an alternative vibe that I'm not sure I fit with. Like I'm the Target to her Glebe Markets. And yet here she is chatting to me, making awful dad jokes.

'So,' I say, looking for another topic of conversation, 'Do you know anyone here?'

I blow on my tea, knowing it will still be too hot to drink. I attempt to take a bite of my pastry. But it is perched on top of my serviette, placed directly on the upturned palm of my hand. I really need to be holding the food in a pincer-like grip. The way I am holding it makes me think that I will look like a dog eating its breakfast if I start to snack on it. I'll have to drink the tea first. *Keep it together, Cleo.*

'I actually don't know anyone here,' says Remi. She sounds surprised and I raise my eyebrow as if to question her. She waves her hand at me like she is brushing off my reaction. 'I've done a few art workshops over the last couple of years. More week-long programs, rather than four-week ones. It's often a similar crowd.' She looks around the people. 'But yeah, this looks like a fresh group.'

'It's not the sort of thing I'm used to going to,' I volunteer.

'No?'

'I guess Oxford Street is not my usual stomping ground,' I say, my voice rising at the end so it sounds like I'm asking a question, even though I don't mean to. I quickly realise what I've said could sound offensive. 'I'm just not from around here. It took almost two hours to get here. I'm from Camden. It's semirural.' *Why did I say the last bit?*

Remi laughs and I know I haven't offended her. 'Isn't Camden in England?'

I nod. 'Yep, and in New South Wales. And probably a bunch of other places.'

'I've been to Camden.' A deeper voice from behind me joins our conversation. I wonder if I am supposed to be impressed that someone knows of the town in which I live. I am about to make a snippy comment but the body belonging to the voice steps closer.

'I'm Lachlan,' the body says. 'I played rugby there . . . last winter, it must have been, not that long ago.'

Lachlan is marginally taller than me. His blond hair is curly but worn short. He looks like a footy player. Strong.

Like he could bench press me. Not that I want him to. I don't think? I don't know why I imagined that. I guess I don't not want him to, either.

'So do you have cows?' he asks.

I pull myself together and try a joke. 'Only half ones, we're *semi*rural.' Oh my gosh, that was awful. Why did I say that? I push on before anyone can comment on my terrible pun. 'Tell me where you guys are from while I figure out how to eat my morning tea.'

I sound more confident than I feel.

Without asking, Lachlan reaches over and takes my tea out of my hand. His fingers skim mine in the exchange. 'Let me help you with that,' he says with a wink.

It's a bold move and I am impressed with his confidence. I smile by way of thanks as he continues. 'I'm from Caringbah. How about you . . .' He flashes a smile at Remi, waiting for her to fill in the blank.

'Remi,' she says. 'I live in Bexley.'

'Nice to meet you, Remi from Bexley,' Lachlan swaps the tea into his left hand and shakes Remi's hand with his right. 'And from Camden is . . .'

This time it's my turn to fill in the blank. 'I'm Cleo.'

'Cleo from Camden. Nice to meet you, Cleo.'

My food is in my right hand but Lachlan takes my left hand anyway and gives it a little squeeze as a makeshift handshake. It could be my imagination, but the squeeze shake lasts marginally longer than it has to. I feel my cheeks beginning to flush and try to cover it by taking a big bite of caramel slice. I have such a sweet tooth and the slice makes me think of baking afternoons with my mum and sister. I push the thought down.

'You guys, this is delicious,' I say, with a half-full mouth. 'You should definitely try it.'

'It's that good?' asks Remi.

I nod emphatically.

'Alright, I'm going in.' Remi ducks away.

Lachlan doesn't move. He passes my tea back to me. Now I only have the pastry in my hand I can hold both comfortably.

'Thanks.'

Lachlan smiles. He looks directly at me, holding my gaze. 'What brings Cleo from Camden here to art school?'

It's not a loaded question and yet there are so many ways to answer it. I like art. I want to learn new techniques. This could help me get a better mark at the end of the year. I need to make some new memories. I don't know what I want to do with my life and I hope this will help me think it through. Or the biggest and most important: the summer I wanted doesn't exist and my parents made me. Welcome to my life, Lachlan, take your pick!

I chew on my pastry and settle on the safest, easiest answer that's the least likely to introduce him to my crazy.

‘Um . . . I guess my art teacher invited me and I thought it’d be fun?’

‘Me too. I’ve got this concept for my major work this year. It’s about muscle growth and development. I was going to use photographs to track a friend’s progress at the gym but my teacher wants me to dig deeper, really think about the why behind it. Consider mixing my mediums. I wasn’t even going to take art. Actually, I thought I’d drop back to ten units, but it’s surprisingly fun.’

‘Yeah, that makes sense,’ I say. I deliberately don’t mention the fact that I agree with his teacher. Conceptually it is a little basic. But who am I to judge? I’m way behind on my major work and still trying to come to terms with what it is I’m trying to do or say.

‘Never thought I’d be drawing nudes though,’ says Lachlan.

There’s a lot to like about Lachlan’s confident, laid-back energy. I can imagine he’s the sort of person at ease in all social situations.

Chatting to Remi and Lachlan is helping settle my nerves and I have almost forgotten the boy I squished next to on the pew. That is until I look over Lachlan’s shoulder and find him staring directly at me.

I look away. A girl can only deal with one new social interaction at a time.

Chapter Two

We're directed to stand in different areas of the quad. Apparently, there are three groups of us. Those here for life drawing (me), printmakers and clay people . . . ceramicists? I think that's the word for it. I concentrate hard to make sure I don't walk with the wrong group. But still I'm shifting my weight from foot to foot, feeling low-level anxious that I am heading in the wrong direction. Luckily Remi is next to me. 'Life drawing, right?'

'You got it.'

'Yep, all of us,' adds Lachlan.

I breathe a sigh of relief. That would have sucked if I had to turn around and make conversation with another bunch of people.

I hate this waiting. The moments in-between. When something new is about to happen and I can't quite imagine what will unfold. It makes me nervous. I scan the courtyard. I see a lady break away from a conversation with Rachael Ramirez. She walks in my group's direction and suddenly, we are moving. I follow the clump of students and concentrate on where we are going. I'm going to need to find my way out again.

Room 10 will be our home during our time here and I love it the moment we walk in. Somehow it feels full of promise. There are windows all around the room, so it's well lit and airy.

While I'm looking at the room, becoming acquainted with it, a handful of students have seized places at the easels which are placed around in a large semicircle. Each easel is turned to a chair placed in the centre of the room. I'm trying to be very adult, but I can't quite fathom the idea that in a little while a stranger will walk into the room and strip down while we watch. It's an odd premise.

Remi heads towards an easel in the middle of the semicircle and I follow her. Around us I can see other students starting to get comfortable. I pull my drink bottle out and take a sip. Then I put it back in my bag. I wonder if I need to get organised. It seems like a good idea. We have been instructed to bring some art materials with us and Miss Saidi helped me collect them from school before the Christmas holidays began. I have an assortment of pencils, charcoal, oil pastels and paintbrushes, and I wonder what we will work with first.

I reach down and get my drink bottle out of my bag again, but leave it at my feet wishing I had a proper table to put my things on.

Maybe if I get my pencil case out it might help me feel ready? I reach down again and take it out. The pencil case looks too big to fit on the edge of the easel so I put it back into my bag and sit up. Remi has a much smaller, neater case and as she rests hers on the edge of the easel, she looks ready. I wonder if my pencil case will fit. I guess it's worth a try? I attempt to balance it on the tiny shelf, but it looks like it's going to fall. Its base is too wide. I hold my hands in front of it, just in case. When it stays put, I breathe a sigh of relief, then worry about the time I wasted focusing on my pencil case. But I know the problem's not really the pencil case. It's this damn in-between time. It's always the moment before the new thing happens that I feel it the most.

I look around the room and see others talking quietly to each other. Some kids look at their phones. Some sit straight, ready for the class. There is a nervous energy and it surprises me to realise that I am not the only person who is feeling uncertain. We are all waiting to see what will happen, waiting to be told what to do.

The woman who has led us here clears her throat. She is small, a little soft around the edges and has tight grey curls. Once she has our attention she smiles and begins. 'Welcome one and all to life drawing. I'm Betty Kenwood and no I am not your model.' This gains a few laughs. 'This is a wonderful program we have for you over the next few weeks. It is lovely to have so many fresh faces. You will be learning a lot during this time. It may surprise you that when you walk out you will not be the same person who walked in. Now to set some ground rules. Working as we do at the easels brings with it many benefits. One of those is seeing each other's work. This may, or may not, be something you feel comfortable with. Let me remind you, we are all on our own art journeys. We all bring to this room different experiences, different skills, different giftings. It should go without saying but I'm going to say it anyway, we will be kind to one another. We will be sharing a lot over this time and it's important that this is a space everyone is happy to be in.'

She looks around the room. There are smiles and nods.

'Good. We are diving straight in this morning and our focus will be on loosening up, relaxing our strokes, building up our confidence. We need to feel at ease to work without thinking, without worrying.'

I feel like she is talking directly to me.

'We will work on some quicker sketches first, so prepare to get messy. Our model will hold her poses for two minutes to begin with, and to ease you in she will keep some layers on. Now without further ado, let me introduce you to Nerida, our first beautiful model.'

Nerida walks in smiling at everyone. She gives us some waves and takes her position on the stool in the middle of our semicircle. Nerida looks to be just older than my mum, but as comfortable as my mum is in her skin, she is nothing compared to the free spirit in front of us. Nerida's hair looks to be transitioning from a warm copper colour into a grey. She is wearing a flowing floral gown which she slides down to reveal shoulders and upper torso. Under her gown I note that she is still wearing a bra and underwear.

'If you don't have your sketchbooks already out, do that now and I'd like you to get out some charcoal to work with,' says Betty. 'It is difficult to keep things neat with charcoal, which is why we are beginning with it. Please give yourself permission to create some chaos on the page. Remember, Nerida will hold each pose for only two minutes and our aim is to work quickly, turning off our minds and just letting our eyes and hands do the work. When I work like this, I almost spend more time looking up than looking at my page.' Betty pauses and looks around at us. 'Now if everyone is ready, we will get started.'

Nerida leans forwards, elbows on her knees, chin cupped in her hands. Her robe slides further down her back. We begin.

I feel movement around me, I can hear soft, fast scratches of charcoal on paper. I have the charcoal in my hand and immediately feel like it is all over me. Charcoal is like germs. Spread from surface to surface with a mere touch. I may be behind but I'm already messy.

I look to my left. Remi is halfway through her sketch. She has started at Nerida's head and is working down. Her strokes seem lightning fast. On my other side, Lachlan has marked in the stool first and is working out from there. I swallow the ball of worry that is sitting in the back of my throat.

Just begin, I tell myself.

I assess Nerida. I'll start with her head, I think. I look up again. Yes, the top is a good place to start. I trace an oval on my paper. Okay, working down. Her neck, no maybe I should fill in her hair. I look at her hair. Okay, time to start shading it in. I'm about to start when Betty claps her hands and I momentarily wonder who Betty is applauding. Then Nerida stands.

Shit.

My first drawing only has one shape on it. Paper rustles around me as everyone turns to their second page. Nerida rests both hands on her hips. A new pose. Her gown is open and we see her whole body. The person to the left of Remi is beginning to mark out the negative space around Nerida. Yeah, okay. That's a good idea.

But is that a good idea? I still think I need to start at the top and work down. I mark out Nerida's head. Great. This sketch looks exactly like my previous one. An oval. I could call it *Oval on a White Page no. 2*. But that's probably not quite what we are going for here. I need to keep drawing, but I can feel my heart racing. I am so far out of my depth here.

Before I capture anything else, Betty claps her hands again and Nerida moves into her third pose. She places her hands on the stool, keeps her arms straight and steps back slightly. I can't even reuse my paper because her head is at a different height. What is wrong with me? Why can't I just start?

Betty, who has been circling the room, stops behind me. My heart picks up again. I don't think I can do this. I can't draw with her behind me.

Betty comes in close.

'You just need to start, don't worry about the outcome,' she whispers to me.

I don't really know how to respond. I nod my head and stare at my blank paper some more. Then after a moment Betty claps her hands again, 'Some great work, everyone,' she says, addressing the whole group. 'I would like us to loosen up even more. I don't want you to be afraid, I don't want you to be stiff. Let's draw this pose again. This time without looking at your page. In fact, let's really make a mess. We're not going to look at our page, we're not going to look at all. For this round everyone will draw with their eyes closed.' I can hear the collective intake of breath. 'It doesn't matter what it looks like. I want to impress this on you. Give yourself permission to let loose. Take one more look . . . Now, eyes closed and draw.'

I follow her instruction.

In my mind I picture Nerida, her weight over the stool, legs straight. Then I follow Betty's advice. Eyes closed; I draw. I lift my charcoal to the paper. I mark out her head, then draw a line for her spine, following it all the way to her toes. I add her arms without worrying whether they meet her shoulders or not. I add the stool then head back up her body to add her hair.

When Betty claps her hands this time, I open my eyes to the sound of soft giggles and whispered exclamations. The page in front of me is no longer empty. My oval series has come to an end. As expected, my page is a mess. Nerida's hair does not frame her face as I imagined I was drawing it. It doesn't even sit like a mop on top of her head. It hovers about ten centimetres off her head, like a strange thought bubble depicting a sour mood. I sneak a look at Remi's easel beside me. She catches my eye and winks. In Remi's sketch Nerida has inherited a carpet of chest hair. Remi mimes brushing invisible chest hair. Laughter rises in me, catching me by surprise.

I look at my work again. It is a mess, there's no mistaking that, but my first long line, Nerida's spine, has been drawn with a confidence that belies my experience.

Betty circles the room. 'Yes!' she cries out. 'This is what I want. Let's do it one more time.'

Nerida stands tall again, her arms stretched long and crossed above her head. I take in her pose, the angles she creates. This time I am ready. I close my eyes and press the charcoal to the page. In my mind I hold the image of Nerida and as I draw, I imagine transferring it to the page. This is an easier pose and I decide not to lift my hand from the page. I try to add details as I go and when Betty claps her hands, I am excited to open my eyes. On my page Nerida now stretches long, the length of her legs, torso and arms all elongated in an exaggerated manner. It is 100% not realistic and yet, I kinda like it. Next to me, Remi gives me a smile. 'Hey, that one really works.'

The warmth of something like pride fills me.

'Thanks. I really loved the second one you did, your shading is incredible.'

Remi smiles at this compliment and as I raise my charcoal ready for the next pose, I realise that this class might not be so traumatic, that it could in fact be sort of wonderful.

Chapter Three

Plan for Conversations

By Emmaline Markson for Cleo Markson

1. *A conversation is just a series of questions and answers. If you can ask questions (and answer them) you can have a conversation. You don't even have to ask good questions!*
   If you've never met, start with: 'What's your name?'
   Follow up with, 'Where are you from?'
   If you have met, ask something like, 'Come here often?'
   Or 'Ever done this before?'
   If you can't think of a question, 'Seen any good shows?' could work.
   Or 'What music are you into?' is also a good backup.
   Note: 'How's the weather?' is a terrible question so only use it if you can't think of ANYTHING else . . .

2. Remember, people love talking about themselves. It's what they know the most about. So, ask them questions about themselves. (Refer back to point one on questions.)
3. Respond to their answer. Let them know what you think about what they said.
For example, 'That's a nice name, how do you spell that?' Failing that, a nod and smile can work at a stretch.
4. It's okay for there to be a pause. The other person needs an opportunity to ask you questions back. It's a bit like tennis (which I know we both don't like, too much grunting) but you serve a question to them, they answer and return it to you with another question. Back and forth it goes until one of you decides they don't want to talk anymore or you both can't think of any more questions.
5. Fake it till you make it. It doesn't matter if you feel like you can't do it. Just pretend that you can. Or imagine you are me!!!! LOL. Love you, little sis.

PS Don't forget, even though you have now mastered the art of conversation, the person talking to you might still suck at it. (They don't have an incredible sister like me to help them.) They might not ask you anything. You might have to do all the heavy lifting. (Have I used too many metaphors here?) But that's okay. Just keep asking them questions. If they are not fidgeting or looking away, they might be happy that they have found someone so interesting/interested in them.

Betty claps her hands and I jump. As Nerida's poses became longer, the frantic energy in the room dissolved, replaced by a new focus. Or perhaps it was just my frantic energy that had dissipated.

After working for only two hours, I have concluded that Betty is a master. She knew exactly what was needed to get us started, or at least to get *me* started, to clear out my nerves. I have been completely absorbed in my sketches.

'You can join me in thanking Nerida,' Betty suggests, holding her hands ready to give Nerida a round of applause, waiting a moment to begin so we can join her. 'We very much appreciate her time today and all she has given us. It's time for a lunch break, and I'll see you back here in an hour's time.'

I step back from my easel and take the time to look at my last drawing. It's not bad. Next to me, Remi is doing the same and Lachlan steps closer to look at mine.

'That was . . .' He pauses, leaving the statement hanging in the air.

I raise my eyebrows at him. 'Different?' I fill in. 'Intense? Incredible?'

'Yes!' Lachlan is nodding and Remi laughs.

'They say you'll always remember your first time,' she says, deadpan, and Lachlan catches my eye before we all dissolve into giggles.

Lachlan reaches over to me and takes my wrist, lifting it closer to him. I don't spend much time around guys and I'm wondering, is it odd that he would just reach out and touch me? But also, is it not odd? Maybe just bold and a little flirty? Or maybe what we've just sat through has bonded us all and I don't need to overcomplicate things. Lachlan lifts my wrist closer. 'It's 12.50 now,' he says, looking at my watch. That's what he is doing, looking at my watch. He could have just asked for the time. Why didn't he just do that? Who is this boy?

'Want to get lunch together?' he asks me and Remi.

'Sound good,' says Remi.

'I'll meet you outside,' I say. 'Just have to go to the loo.'

It's been a huge morning. New people and new places. And I need a couple of minutes to regroup before heading out to lunch. Also, what was with the hand thing?

It's totally unsurprising that I have never had a boyfriend. Despite this fact I have somehow managed to catalogue all the physical contact I've had with boys over the years. My list is very short, very sad and honestly, if I was anyone else, I probably wouldn't have listed some of the moments. But here you have it.

- In year 7, Markus Kovac knocked me over in the hallway because he was running to keep up with his friends. It was highly embarrassing.

He came back a minute later and said, 'Sorry. I hope you're okay,' and he kind of patted my shoulder awkwardly. I think the maths teacher made him apologise.

- In year 8, Blake Green touched the small of my back before I went onstage in the school production. I don't think he was pushing me. It was more of a *good luck, go well* moment. It stuck in my mind, and I remember it to this day.
- In PE last year we did a dance unit. Someone from swimming told me they got to learn a hip-hop routine, but my school seems stuck in the 1950s so I learned the cha-cha and the jive with Daniel Heng. At the start of the unit, our teacher told us to pair up. It was one of those moments where we just ended up together because we were both left in the last group of twenty or so kids who were too embarrassed to ask anyone to dance with them. He kind of just looked at me and I nodded and we spent the time literally not saying anything to each other and dropping each other's hands as soon as we'd mastered the dance steps. There was absolutely no prolonged contact.
- In the summer of year 12, just now, Lachlan grabbed my wrist to look at the time.

That's it. That's the list, short and sad as described.

I give myself a pep talk in the mirror while I wash my hands. I don't say it out loud like they do in the movies – you know, so we have access to their inner monologues.

It's new, and that's okay. In fact, it's more than okay. This is a great experience in a new place with new people and it's been pretty good so far, actually pretty great.

I nod at myself. *You've got this.*

I head back out and stop immediately. In the course of pepping myself up I have forgotten which way I am supposed to walk to get out of the building. Do I go left, or right? Crappity crap.

I turn left and start walking before realising that is the way back to the classroom. I stop and turn 180 degrees. Yes, this is the way out. I've taken about ten steps when I realise that I was right the first time. I let out an audible groan and whirl around again only to stop immediately.

Matt/Matthew/Matteo is standing right in front of me. The boy I shared a pew with is looking at me with a bemused expression spread across his ridiculously attractive face. His hair is a warm chestnut colour and he has it fairly long over his forehead. His eyes are green with dark lashes. He is much taller than me and his shoulders are as broad as I would have guessed after sitting squished next to him.

It's funny, if I wasn't as rushed this morning there is no way I would have sat next to him. I am not the sort of person who gravitates towards attractive people. I have a theory that people tend to connect with others who are of roughly the same level of attractiveness as they are. Take for example friendship groups at school. People group with like-looking people. While I don't have a definitive answer as to why they do this, my working theory is that perhaps the pretty people are worried that poor bone structure or less than ideal cheekbones and eye size might somehow rub off on them.

Or maybe it's just because those of us whose looks aren't good enough to turn heads or stop traffic don't need the daily reminder of what we are missing.

All this to say, one thing you can count on is that I don't sit with the beautiful people. Or even the obviously talented people, come to think of it. My friends are great but no one else really knows our little group of three. I think there must be some sort of sliding scale. Maybe you get added points for charisma or intelligence or talent? Like how the most popular boy at school is not always the hottest? They might still be good looking but if they are far and away the best soccer player at school then they clean up in the point scale.

My school point scale is way down but my sister's points were so high it felt like people just deducted points from me simply because I wasn't her.

But this guy standing in the hallway? He's not even on the scale.

And now I'm standing in the hallway looking at this gorgeous boy, thinking about point scales, and he's looking at me and I'm looking back at him and it feels like he should have said something. But he hasn't, and I've clearly been having way too many thoughts, so I haven't either.

What is even going on right now?

No word has been spoken but he seems to be questioning me with his eyes and I am unable to come up with a good answer.

I think about the plan for conversations. I need to ask a question.

Come on, Cleo, ask a question.

'What?'

It is a question. But not a very good one and I sound slightly pissed, which is probably *mostly* unfair but this hallway stand-off has me feeling weird and I am now considering deducting points from him for not having the decency to say hello after we sat next to each other.

'Where are you going?' he asks and even though it's a better question than mine I frown because I know where I need to be but can't quite remember how to get there.

'I'm going out to lunch,' I say.

'Then why are you heading back to the art room? Did you leave something there?'

I consider this for a moment. I haven't left anything in there, except perhaps my dignity, and I consider my two options.

Option One: telling him, *Yes, just have to grab something* and then going back in the room to save face.

Option Two: admitting I have no idea where I am.

In the end, my desire to leave the building and have lunch with Remi and Lachlan overrides my desire not to feel like a moron so I tell the truth.

'Nope, didn't leave anything,' I say. 'Just in the process of getting lost.' I give my head a little scratch. 'Are you heading out?'

'Yeah, pretty sure the door is just down here,' and I swear as he says it the corner of his mouth twitches.

And yes, of course the door is.

He holds it open.

'Thanks.' I want to say something else, but I don't think of anything fast enough and before I can come up with anything he gives me a wave.

'See you after lunch,' he says as I head over to meet Remi and Lachlan.

'Who was that?' asks Lachlan.

'I'm not actually sure,' I say. 'Maybe Matt? He's in our class.'

Lachlan raises his eyebrows. 'Cool. Hey, let's get some food, I'm starving.'

Moments later we are seated at the Art School cafe. I am stoked with my $6 salad. Where else can you buy a $6 salad? My sister would be impressed. Not that it matters. I shake my head, a physical attempt to get the thoughts to leave.

Remi has also opted for the salad and Lachlan chomps on a hash brown and egg roll.

I brace myself for the inevitable question. The question everyone asks students in year 12. Ever wondered what the most common conversation for a year 12 student is, particularly when said student is talking to an adult? Wonder no longer. People just love to ask: *What are you going to do next year?*

I feel like this is an impossible question. Because seriously, how can I be expected to know the answer to it? I can't foretell what mark I'm going to get. And even if I could, I have no idea if I want to go university, because I don't know what I want to study. And even if I did know what I wanted to study, who's to say that a tree won't fall on our house in the middle of the night, killing me and rendering the question irrelevant? No one. Or that the thing I thought I wanted to do isn't going to be torn away from me? That can't be guaranteed either. Nothing is guaranteed.

So, my answer now is always the same. *I don't know.*

It's not a particularly satisfactory answer. And it often leads to further lines of inquiry that are equally frustrating, all designed to help me answer the original question. Like they are determined to find the solution to my problem.

What do you like? What are you good at? What can you imagine yourself being?

Good questions. Sensible questions. Valid questions. Questions I can almost answer but can't quite be translated into something that solves . . . well, anything really.

Surprisingly, the question doesn't come; neither Remi nor Lachlan bring it up.

Instead, Remi asks, 'Do you get much of a chance to work on your art at home?' while dusting the corner of her mouth with a serviette.

'Not really,' says Lachlan. 'It's more of a school thing for me. I guess I'm spending a lot of time on the field, or in the gym.'

I follow up with another question, derived from the answer he gave. 'What type of field?'

'Rugby and cricket mostly. I'm the wicketkeeper.'

And just like that, I have no more follow-ups, so I redirect the original question to Remi. 'How 'bout you, Remi? Do you have a home project you're working on?'

'Sure do, but I wish I had more time, you know? My mum's taken on a new role at work so I'm on call a bit with my brother.'

'The one who wakes eye-wateringly early?' I ask.

'Yep, that's the one. Mum can't always pick him up from school so it's on me a bit. Dad died when I was younger,' she adds.

I look away. I can't believe she just said it out loud like that.

'Wow, sorry,' says Lachlan, while I try to work out how to react.

'No, no, I didn't say it for sympathy,' she says matter-of-factly, like it's not one of the most devastating things to happen. 'It was a long while ago now, and I do miss him. I really do, but I don't like to dwell. Not too often, anyway.' She waves her fork at Lachlan. 'So, who's in your house, Lachlan? You said you're in Caringbah; that must be nice, to live so close to the beach.'

'It's a good corner of the world,' agrees Lachlan. 'We haven't always lived there. We were a bit further south when I was younger, still on the coast though. I feel like I grew up outside, you know. In the sun or the sand,' he says before taking another bite and chewing it thoughtfully. When he starts again, my mind begins to spin because they are going to ask me the same question and I'm not sure how to answer. 'My mum would take me and my brothers – I've got two brothers,' he adds in. 'She'd take us to the beach whenever she needed a break. My brothers and me are all really active, so she needed a break a lot. She let us run around, and swim, till we were tired out.'

'Sounds idyllic,' says Remi, while my mind still spins. 'If a little intense.'

'It was,' says Lachlan, smiling at me, his eyes crinkling at the edges. Still focused on me, he asks, 'What about you, Cleo? Who's at home with you?'

I still don't know what to say, but I can't sit here mute. 'There's me and my mum and dad . . .' I say, then pause. I'm not quite sure how to say it. This might be the first time I've had to say it to someone who doesn't know. How do I say it?

'Cool,' says Lachlan jumping in before I finish my sentence. Remi was so open with her answer, and I should explain my situation too. I'm about to speak when a pop beat fills the airwaves. It's like the serving staff have just turned it up.

'Oh my gosh, I love this song,' says Remi.

It takes me a minute before I recognise it. 'I wouldn't have picked you for a Mariah Carey fan,' I say with a chuckle.

I imagined Remi would be into some indie band I had never heard of.

'The fact that you know this is Mariah tells me more than you think,' says Remi, singing along, using her spoon as a microphone.

'You've got to love the old stuff,' says Lachlan, picking up his spoon.

As the music hits its crescendo, Remi holds the spoon out to me. I surprise myself by singing along – Lachlan joins me and what he lacks in skill he makes up in commitment.

When the song ends, we fall about laughing.

'Music buddies and art buddies!' says Lachlan. It's more of a statement than a question and I love his certainty and confidence.

It feels good to be part of something.

I'll tell them later, I decide. I don't want to bring things down.

Chapter Four

'Welcome back, everyone.' Betty glances around the room. 'So glad I haven't lost anyone. In our first class, it's important to dive straight in. I really like to give you a feel for what we are doing straight away. But in our second session, I like to relax things a bit more, help you feel more comfortable.'

Yes please, Betty!

'We are going to do some exercises drawing our own hands and our feet. But before we do that, I'd love for you to all step out from behind your easels.'

No one moves.

'Let's do it, out you all come.'

Lachlan smiles at me and Remi nods and I am thankful to have already found my crew, otherwise this would have felt so much harder. We join the rest of the group, who are shuffling sheepishly to the front of their easels to stand in a semicircle, eyes darting up at each other. 'It's so easy to hide away with this set up,' says Betty. 'But we are not drawing alone in our garages, locking ourselves and our art away. This is the time for community and encouragement. For sharing ourselves and our art. So, let's start to get to know each other.'

I'm listening to Betty, but at the same time I can't help but notice Matt, Matthew, Matteo standing at the edge of the circle. He is not looking around the room but rather concentrating only on Betty's instructions. He nods his head slightly as Betty lists what she wants us to tell the group.

I'm still looking at Matt when Betty starts. 'As you know, my name is Betty and I teach at the Australian Art School. My favourite medium is, as you might have guessed, charcoal. I love its mess and the freedom it brings. And something else I love is taking Harriett, my rescue greyhound, for walks.' I can't help but smile at the image that brings to mind, a short round woman with a tall skinny dog. I'm still smiling when Betty gestures with her hand towards Matt/Matthew/Matteo to go next. He looks round at the group and I feel like his eyes meet mine and pause before he begins, but I could be imagining it.

'I'm Mattias,' he says drawing out the syllables, *Matt – tee – us*. Huh, there you go. 'Although, some people call me Matt. I go to school in Heathcote. I like working with pastels and I love Illawarra flame trees.' He nods as he says this, as if sealing the truth of the statement and daring anyone to question it. Then he looks to the girl on his left, passing an imaginary baton along, telling her that it is her turn. The girl is wearing black jeans and a worn black t-shirt with what I can only assume is a band name scrawled across the front. Her lip is pierced. She scares me a little.

'I'm Imogen, I go to school in Parramatta and I like water colours and musicals.' I feel my eyes widen slightly. That is not what I expected her to say. Suddenly I am intrigued.

Next is Amina, who is from Kellyville, then Kiaan, who loves robotics, which strikes me as odd because shouldn't he be at some STEM day if that's what he loves? And then it is Lachlan, who is clearly comfortable holding a room.

'I'm Lachlan and I love long walks on the beach.' The class groans collectively. Lachlan flashes a big smile and wins everyone back. 'I go to a sports high school in Caringbah and actually I'm normally into photography, but if I'm not hiding behind a lens,' – seriously, I'm pretty sure this boy never hides from anything – 'then I guess pencil is good for me. What else? I do love the beach, love surfing, sailing, diving.' Lachlan turns to me and touches my shoulder. 'Tag, you're up, Cleo.'

And suddenly everyone is looking at me.

'Uh, hi, I'm Cleo. I go to school in Camden. I like pencil too, it's easiest to rub out.' I've now exposed my insecurities to the whole group. 'And . . .' Crap, I was so busy listening to everyone else that I'm not sure what to say. 'I don't know, I love . . .' My brain is whirling, do I say a TV show? No, that's lame. I don't have a pet to mention. I work at a pool and like swimming, but that will seem too similar to Lachlan. Why can't I think of something cool, that sums up my personality in one clever line? Everyone's eyes are on me . . . I glance over at Mattias, and think about trees with vibrant red leaves, which sparks something in me. 'I love jacaranda trees. The purple flowers against a blue or grey sky . . . just beautiful.' Okay, stop there, no more. I look to Remi. It's over.

'I'm Remi, I'm at school in Kogarah, I'm enjoying acrylics at the moment and I love learning new things.' Remi is poised and smart; what a great answer.

Around the circle, each student has a turn introducing themselves until we get back to Betty. 'Wonderful to meet you all. Now you know each other, please don't hide. I've found friendships formed at these workshops to be long-lasting. Right, get comfortable, we are going micro now, looking at little details, but we'll have some fun doing it. I'd like you to get your stool and move it to the other side of your easel, so we are back in this circle together. Grab your sketchbooks too, as we will be using them now.'

Betty takes us through a series of exercises drawing our hands and our feet. She makes us draw without lifting our pencils, without taking our eyes off our feet, and in our non-dominant hands. After each drawing, we hold the sketch up for the class to see. After the first one, I can see some people's hesitancy matches my own, but as the most ridiculous sketches seem to get the biggest cheers, I feel far more comfortable.

After working through this process, we begin taking our time. Betty encourages us to look for the tiny details and make sure we incorporate these into our pieces. Then calm descends on the room, our energy settling right down. We are not silent the way we were with Nerida; rather, soft conversations drift around the room.

'I like this,' I say to Remi.

'Me too.'

I feel like the pressure is off and my mind wanders. I wonder what Emmy would make of this, of me, sitting with a group of people I have only just met connecting, creating. She'd be proud, I think. *'I've taught you well,'* she'd say, taking the credit, giving me a little nudge. Because that was what she always did: give me little nudges, figuratively helping me move forward, helping me get through whatever I was finding hard and cheering me on when things went well.

Emmy moved through life differently to me. It seemed like she glided through easily, where life for me was like wading through mud, or walking a maze. I didn't do it so elegantly and I was always thankful when she reached her hand out. She wasn't perfect, obviously. But that was our dynamic. It was like rather than letting me constantly annoy her, as lots of little sisters do, she decided she'd help me out. Maybe she saw me as a project? I'm not sure. But either way, she had time for me.

Together we'd make plans. Perhaps 'together' is a bit of a stretch. *She'd* make plans for *me*, how-to guides, essentially. 'We can plan our way through everything,' she'd say.

She wrote me so many plans and I knew that she was the one to listen to, to follow. I looked up to her. I wouldn't be the same person without her. I was closer to her than anyone else. She was my best friend.

I pause, putting my pencil down and pulling my phone out. I know she's not going to answer, can't answer, but I text her anyway.

Emmy, I wish you were here. I made new friends today. I'd love to tell you all about it.

I wait, hoping to see the three little dots pulsing on the screen meaning she had read the message and was going to respond, before reminding myself it won't happen. It isn't possible. I slide my phone back into my pocket and go back to sketching my ankle.

*

Beginning new things in new places has always been a bit of a thing for me. For some, a fresh start brings a sense of excitement, a sense of possibility. Not so for me. It makes me nervous. I can't remember what starting school was like, but my mum informs me that in the time leading up to it I asked her hundreds of questions. How will I know what to do? How will I know who my teacher is? How will I know how to make friends? How will I know who to make friends with? How will I know what the bells mean? How will I know where to go? She says the questions didn't stop till I'd experienced it myself. Her answers to them were never enough. She says it was like asking the questions was my attempt to understand what I was heading into, to imagine it in my head so that when I experienced it I felt less out of my depth, more in control. I don't remember any of this. My only memory of beginning kindergarten is fleeting. I can visualise my shiny, slightly tight and not at all worn-in black school shoes walking across the rough asphalt. I can see my brand-new school bag. White, with red and orange butterflies on it. But I can't remember anything else.

What I do remember is the lead up to high school. I remember the sense of apprehension that set in in term four of year 6. While the rest of my grade talked excitedly about the schools they were going to, I tried to pretend that year 7 was something that wouldn't happen to me. When relatives or friends' parents asked me if I was excited, I shook my head and changed the subject. Of course, I knew I couldn't escape year 7, that my wishes or my worry wouldn't halt the passing of time, but denial is a fine thing.

One week before the school year began, my mum took my sister and me to buy new school uniforms. My sister had grown and needed new everything. I was going to get her hand-me-downs, but Mum wanted to get me one new set too. She felt it was important I had one that belonged only to me. I did not agree. I was happy to use my sister's old uniforms. The material felt softer. They were worn-in by the two years she had spent in high school while I finished primary school. I had the sense that if I wore the old clothes, my sister's experience of high school might somehow rub off on me. They also made me look like I fit in. Brand-spanking-new uniforms always marked their wearers in a certain way. They signified a lack of experience, they screamed to the rest of the community, 'Look at me! I'm just starting out. I'm new!' I did not want to send that message. If I had to go to high school, I wanted to blend in. I didn't want the crisp folds of my stark white button-down to draw any attention to me. I preferred the off-white shirt that had gone through the wash an immeasurable number of times. But somehow I couldn't quite work out how to articulate this to my mum, and so we found ourselves in the uniform shop, me locked in a change room with my sister and mum waiting outside.

Every time I think back on this, I feel like the ultimate drama queen, and yet I know the emotions were real. I had been feeling sick on the way there, my stomach was uneasy and before we even looked at the uniforms I had to use the bathroom. When I got back Mum had a pile of ladies size 8 to 10s ready to go. As I buttoned up my blouse and straightened my knee-length skirt, my thoughts began to race through all the questions that Mum said I had asked about kindy. Plus, some added extras. How will I know what to do? How will I know who to make friends with? How will I know what the bells mean? What if the bell goes and I forget to go to period 2 and go out and start eating my recess instead? What if I don't know where to go? What if I walk into the wrong classroom? What if I get lost?

'Cleo?' Mum's voice sang out from behind the door. 'How are you going? Show us how it looks.'

'Not good, Mum,' I choked out. The questions continued to race through my mind. *What if I get into trouble and I didn't even know what the rule I broke was? What if I can't keep up with the rest of my class? What if the rest of my class can't keep up with me?* I was starting to panic. I didn't think to open the door.

My sister's head appeared under the cubicle. 'I'm coming through, Cleo,' she told me. 'You're okay.' She lay flat on her front on the dusty shop floor and started wiggling under. 'I'm here, you're not alone.' She had made it to my side. She wrapped an arm around me.

I wonder now if it was a panic attack, or if my memory is distorted by my sister's heroism, if, had she waited a moment longer, I would have opened the door and it would have been fine. I remember her whispering, 'I've always wanted to squeeze under the door like that. I wasn't sure if I could fit, but now I know I can.'

It made me giggle.

'I know you're worried,' she said, wrapping her arm around my shoulders, 'but you will be fine, you'll see. You just have to get started. The start is always the hard part. You know that.'

I nodded, because I did know that.

'And I'll help you, you'll see.'

And because she was my sister and because I had always wanted to be her and because she looked so calm, so resolute, so sure, I believed her. She smiled in encouragement then helped me up and unlocked the door. My mum wrapped her arms around the both of us. 'Oh, my girls,' she said. 'What a blessing to have each other.'

We left without buying the uniform I tried on and without my sister's new uniform. Mum bundled us into the car and then made us both hot Milos even though it was 32 degrees outside.

I was sitting on my bed drinking my Milo, re-reading my favourite graphic novel, when I heard a knock on the door. 'Yes,' I called but no one entered. Instead, a folded A4 piece of paper slide slid under the door to my room. I remember thinking how much easier it was for paper to slide under a door than it was for a 14-year-old.

I read it straight away.

Plan for Starting Somewhere New

By Emmaline Markson for Cleo Markson (if she wants it)
If starting somewhere new feels too much, then following these plans might be of some help to you.

1. *Focus on the things within your control.*
    a. *Wear something comfortable. (I know you have to wear a uniform to school, but pick the one you like the best, even if Mum thinks it's looking scrappy.)*
    b. *Pack a lunch you want to eat. Even if you don't know where to sit at lunch/recess, having something you like will make you feel better. (Maybe even pack a special snack? We could make those Nutella biscuits you like??)*
    c. *Take a book with you. That way you can look busy if you need to.*
2. *Familiarise yourself with the location/school as much as you can ahead of time. (See map attached, it's from my old diary.)*
3. *Know where the bathrooms are. (See point two to help with this, also I have highlighted them for you and numbered them. Stay away from number 5 if you aren't into vapes, I'm not, I assume you won't be either.)*
4. *Put something small in your pocket that feels reassuring to hold. If things feel too much then you can hold/stroke/squeeze/play with the item. (Not sure if this will work but it's maybe worth a try?)*
5. *If you can, try to smile – a fake-it-till-you-make-it strategy. Also, smiling apparently releases dopamine, serotonin and endorphins into your body. These are good hormones and will actually make you feel happier!!!*
6. *Take deep breaths, even if you have to repeat 'breath in, breath out' in your mind. It might sound stupid, but it could help.*

7. *Here's another idea, it's something I like to do. Every day at the same time, I take a minute to stop. I look up at the sky and remember how big the world is. It helps give me some sort of perspective, if I'm not feeling great.*
8. *Remember: you've got this and you've got me, always. Text me if you need me, but you won't!*

This list was so Emmy. It made me laugh, it almost made me cry and with it I knew I'd be fine, even if it was hard at the start. I knew other kids who couldn't stand their siblings. They had been forced to promise not to say hello to their older brothers and sisters at high school. They were instructed to ignore them if their paths ever crossed. I was so grateful for a sister who had my back. Who had promised to look after me. I felt that because Emmy was so smart, so kind, I might just be able to make it through.

Looking back, I realise that she must have spent some time researching, but at the time I assumed that she knew about everything. She always seemed to know everything. My sister, who wouldn't let a silly thing such as a locked change room door get between us.

Chapter Five

When I walk through my front door, I feel a strange mix of exhaustion and exhilaration. It has been a big day filled with unknowns. So many different scenarios that could have played out differently but didn't. I spent the train and bus trip home replaying the day over in my head. When my alarm went off I paused and looked out the window, drawing on an older memory, but for most part of the journey I was enjoying thinking about the little moments in the day and storing details away.

I wish again that my sister was around so I could share my stories with her. If she was, I would snuggle under the covers at the foot of her bed, and tell her all about the people I met, about Remi and Lachlan and his easy nature and Betty and the beautiful Nerida. But she is not home, she hasn't been home for a long time, and knowing that I can't share my day dims my mood considerably.

My house is a single-storey four-bedroom red brick house. It's not super modern, nor does it feel particularly old. Mum has been keen to redo the interior – to get rid of the deep maroon feature wall in the lounge room and purchase some new furniture – but Dad has been saving for their Europe trip, so Mum's plans have been put on the backburner.

I head towards the kitchen that Mum refers to as 'messier than I would like' and Dad calls 'lived in'. Unsurprisingly, Mum is sitting at the table. The kitchen has always been our house's hub, where all the important things happen. Mum looks up from the table, where she has been flicking through one of those free supermarket magazines full of recipes that look easy but require lists of ingredients no one ever keeps in their pantry. I can tell Mum is itching to ask me about my day. Sitting at the table, she is ready to intercept as soon as I come in. But she plays it cool. 'Good day, hun?'

I can practically feel her holding her questions in. I know she has deliberately chosen this closed question which allows me the space to answer in one word or provide her with all the detail she so desires.

I choose a one-word answer. 'Yeah.' I'm not sure I'm quite ready to spill all the details to her just yet. I open the fridge and rummage around for something to eat. Even with the door open, I can feel her eyes boring into me.

'Your father and I have already eaten. There's some veggie lasagne in there for you too if you want it.' She looks down and casually turns a page like she hasn't just attempted to extract information with a look alone.

'Thanks, Mum.'

Mum manages to contain herself while I reheat the lasagne and fill a glass with water. She continues flicking while I take my place on the other side of the table.

After a big sip of water, I finally cave. 'Want to see what we did today?'

My mother's face lights up. 'Yes of course, I thought you'd never ask.' She transforms from ice queen to eager beaver. 'But in case your father asks, you'll tell him I played it very cool, right? Now, shall I get it from your bag?'

'Yes, Mum.' I answer two questions at once and go back to eating the lasagne.

Dad has been encouraging Mum to give me space. But if I'm being completely honest, I appreciate Mum's consistent presence. It'll never make up for the gap left but I'm thankful for her, not that I'd ever tell her.

Mum has my sketchbook and is looking through the work I have done. She pauses at each page, silently assessing it before giving me her feedback.

'These are fantastic, Cleo. They definitely get stronger as they go along.'

'Well, considering the first two are ovals only and the next couple look pretty demented, I'm glad you can see my progress.'

Mum looks up at my face, judging how to take this comment and I decide to help her out. 'I found it hard to start,' I say, 'but I got going in the end.'

Mum pauses at the one of Nerida standing straight, arms stretched above her head, one hand clasped around the other wrist. 'This one. This one is my favourite so far.'

'Why that one?'

'I'm not sure . . . I think it's the pose. And somehow, you've captured a spirit of total boldness, yet vulnerability too.'

'I mean there's like ten lines max there, Mum. I don't know if you can read that much into it.'

'Weren't you the one who said it was the artist's job to create meaning and the audience's job to find their own meaning? I stand by what I said: boldness and vulnerability. A bit like you.'

This conversation is a little deeper than I'd like it to be.

'Okay, thanks, Mum, I'll take that.' I stand and swipe my sketchbook back from Mum and place it in my bag.

'It's really good, darling,' she says. 'You know, that would make a fantastic birthday gift. Especially if it was set in a nice raw timber frame. Just in case anyone's birthday is coming up . . .' She trails off as I stifle a smile. Mum's fiftieth is coming up at the end of the month and she hasn't been shy in her present hints.

'I'll keep that in mind,' I say, making a mental note because it's a great idea, even though I hope I will have something better to frame by the end of the program.

There's a pause in our conversation and then Mum asks, 'So your summer plans are working out?' To an outsider this might sound like an innocent question, but I know the intent that sits beneath the surface. The word 'plans' hangs in the air between us and I decide not to dignify the question with an answer. I ignore it and keep eating my lasagne.

Mum can't let it go though. 'I'm glad you went, we are so proud of you, darling. It's good to move on.'

This is what Dad means about space. I'm glad she is there, but sometimes the woman is like a dog with a bone.

I roll my eyes and drain my water glass in one go. I place my knife and fork together on my plate and take it and my glass over to the sink. I open the dishwasher and, noting that it's full and clean, I close it again. Normally I'd unpack it straight away but I really don't want to give Mum more opportunity to needle me. I leave my dish in the sink. I don't want to have this conversation now.

'Night, Mum.'

The thing is, I didn't plan to go. I was selected, nominated, invited, whatever you want to call it. That happened and so I went – more cause and effect, I guess. The reason Mum's question irks me so much is that planning and I have a complicated history. Plans have lulled me into a false sense of security; they whispered to me that I could indeed conquer each new mountain, urged me onwards, upwards. That was their job, what they were made to do. But plans and planning have also let me down, allowed me to fall without a safety net. Because the plans I have only lead me up to the end of the year and after that I'm on my own. Next year, when school finishes, is when everything changes, and I'm afraid. I don't have any plans for next year and I don't know what I want to do and the way I would normally approach this situation is not a possibility anymore. It's an endless sprawl of the unknown and I have to manage it without the help of the person who knows me best. Quite frankly, I don't want to think about it.

Mum's comment has me reeling and I want a distraction. I need to think about something different. In my room I flop onto my bed and scroll on my phone. I like the pictures of Amber and Sadie, my friends from school, holidaying together in Burleigh Heads, but I don't comment on them. I don't know what to say. It'd be easy to be jealous that I didn't get the invite, but if I'm really honest with myself I'm not sure I would have gone. It's been harder and harder to find things to talk about with them and I get the sense they don't quite know what to do with me anymore, so when they fessed up and told me that's what they were doing for most of the holidays, it felt like a bit of a relief. After liking their happy snaps, I attempt to locate my new friends online. Remi is pretty easy to find; she told me her handle when we were talking art projects.

Remi's page is full of beautiful photography of completely random things. A snail's path shining in the sun, a street sign, a pot plant, and some market shots, artwork. Things she likes, things she sees the beauty in. It feels completely her. After going through and liking her images, I search for Lachlan. He has a large number of followers, which feels simultaneously surprising (because of the number) and completely unsurprising. A testament to his popularity. Lachlan's images are full of smiling beautiful people, sport shots and beach pics. A girl whose insta handle is @sunnydayz2230 appears with a frequency that makes my stomach drop. In each shot her eyes twinkle and her smile is carefree. Her cleavage is prominent and her confidence is always visible. Her vitality is overwhelming. I try to imagine what I would look like in the pictures, his arm slung around my shoulder, pulling me closer than anyone else. His face up against mine, my long honey-coloured hair spilling over his shoulders (it's somehow behaving perfectly in the imaginary picture), my brown eyes shining, looking towards Lachlan and not the photographer, my mouth open in a laugh, like someone has captured us in a candid moment. Could I be that confident?

I find myself reading through the comments with more interest than I care to admit. He's obviously a bit of a player, of course he is. But maybe I can learn something from him?

Once I've finished stalking Lachlan, I consider attempting to find Mattias but realise that I don't even know his last name, so I discard the idea as pointless.

Chapter Six

The trip in doesn't feel quite as epic the second time I take it. I'm not checking my phone and looking out the window for location clues every two minutes.

Arriving at the entrance of the Art School, I hear a voice behind me.

'You're early today.'

I can't place the voice and when I turn around, I see Mattias.

'*I* was early yesterday too,' I say, before I can stop myself. 'It was my *bus* that was late.'

'That's sure to hold up in court.'

I don't know what to say to that and there's a pause. And then it's awkward again. We walk about ten more paces and I realise that even though we've introduced ourselves in a class setting, he's still essentially a stranger.

'I'm Cleo,' I say. 'We haven't properly met.' Despite the fact that our thighs are well acquainted. 'It's Mattias, right?'

'Yes, Mattias.' He says it slowly. *Matt-tee-us*, drawing out the syllables so I know how to pronounce it.

'Do you have to do that a lot?' I ask.

'Every time I say my name.'

'Names can be so tricky. My dad's a teacher and he's told me more than once about the stress of reading the roll for a new class, knowing that he will mispronounce someone's name at some point. He always apologises at the start and promises to get it right the second time. But there are names spelt with traditional spellings and non-traditional pronunciations, then there are the names that are familiar but are spelt differently, he says those are a major trap for the young and uninitiated, and then there are names he's never come across before. He always says, "It's a game you can't win."' I'm rambling now and tell myself to stop.

'Right . . .' says Mattias. I pray for him to move the conversation on, but he is giving me nothing. My rambling has clearly freaked him out.

We walk the rest of the way inside in silence.

Remi is already there, so I head over to her and dump my bag on the floor.

In a move that makes no sense to me, Mattias pulls up the chair next to mine. Does he want to encourage more awkward conversations that go nowhere?

Remi thankfully looks happy to see me. 'How was your trip in today? Feel more on top of it?'

'Yep, and the bus wasn't late, so I'm here with time to spare.' I give Mattias a pointed look when I say this.

When the morning's model enters the room, I find it impossible not to stare. If I had to guess, I'd say he is about ten years older us and even though he wears a loose cotton tee and a pair of linen shorts it's not hard to see he has an incredible, almost Hemsworthian body. If Emmy were here, she would be wiggling her eyebrows at me, a wicked grin across her face. She loved the God of Thunder.

His hair is red and tied back in a topknot. It feels like an odd thing to say, because he's literally here to be our model, but he *looks* like a model. I can imagine him sauntering down a runway at Paris Fashion Week. He blows Betty a kiss as she welcomes us back.

'I hope your night was restorative and you feel ready to create again,' Betty says to the class. We have all resumed our positions at our easels and are listening in the eager way of people ready to learn. 'In an effort to keep things loose, to take away any feelings of self-consciousness' – I swear she is speaking directly into my heart – 'we will do our first few sketches of our model in our non-dominant hand. This here is Jesse. I hope you will make him feel at home.' To be honest, with this man's level of confidence I have no doubt he would feel at home in every possible scenario, but along with everyone in the class I make a show of nodding and smiling at Jesse.

'Short poses to begin with, then we will head into some longer ones. Remember: non-dominant hand for our first few.'

Jesse stretches his right arm up, bicep flexing as he grabs the back of his collar. At least half of the class audibly sighs as he pulls his shirt off over his head and takes his first pose, hands interlocked behind his head, biceps still flexed. Jesse's pectorals are defined and his stomach is flat with abdominals clearly outlined. His is the body of someone who knows its way around a gym. In and of itself, it is a work of art.

With my charcoal stick in my right hand, my non-dominant hand, I begin to sketch. The fear doing a bad job does not consume me, though it is hovering close by.

The results are nothing to write home about, but they achieve their purpose. I am feeling looser, more confident in my marks. After three poses, Betty claps her hands and nods at Jesse. 'We are moving into six-minute poses now,' she says to both Jesse and us. Then she speaks to the class directly. 'You may swap hands again.'

'Let's do this,' says Remi, flipping the charcoal into her right hand and twirling it around her fingers.

Lachlan gives his head a couple of rolls and jumps up and down on the spot as if he is limbering up for a race. He gives me a thumbs up.

Ready to start, I look up to check Jesse's new position. He is seated on the stool, back hunched, elbows on knees face resting on his hands. But – what the heck? Where are his shorts?

While we swapped hands, Jesse had a costume change, slipping discreetly out of his shorts and straight into his birthday suit.

And oh my, he is now fully naked in the middle of the room. Has anyone else registered how bizarre this moment is, or are we all pretending that this is a normal, ordinary moment? I check my classmates. How is no one phased by the very beautiful and very naked man in the room?

Get it together, Cleo. You can do this.

Right.

I start at the top of his body and work down. It's not too bad because he has one knee up. I keep working until Betty claps her hands. Jesse changes position again and holy hell! I can see his penis.

There it is, hanging right in front of me.

Meat and two vege, out for all to see.

Why is no one else fussed about this?

Get it together, Cleo. I repeat the day's mantra. *You can do this.*

I flip the page and start again. I draw his head, neck, shoulders, arms, torso, legs, feet. I'm so absorbed in what I am doing I don't hear Betty until she is right beside me. 'I think you might be missing an important detail.' In my sketch, Jesse resembles a Ken doll. His nether region is very smooth.

'You still have time,' says Betty, looking at her watch. 'Keep your eyes on him, draw what you see.' But I can't bring myself to look directly at Jesse's, ahem, manhood, and I feel the heat in my cheeks, so I make a quick mark on my page. Ken crisis averted.

I take a quick peek at Remi's sketch. Her style is fluid and relaxed, she is shading as she goes, rather than just outlining. I look back at my work.

Oh crap.

There appears to be one major difference between our sketches and it's nothing to do with shading. It's a problem of ratio.

Remi notices me comparing and glances at mine. The corners of her mouth turn up. 'I know it's bad,' I say and try to laugh it off. 'Thor's hammer just got a whole lot bigger.'

Remi's giggle-snort draws Lachlan's attention. He looks over. 'Is Thor able to wield that weapon?' he quips.

'It's so wrong,' I say. 'I know, I know. I'll um, I'll fix it.'

Before I get the chance, Betty claps her hands. 'Longer poses now,' she instructs. 'Take your time.'

'For what it's worth, I'm not sure Thor would be upset by your drawing,' Lachlan says, his eyes crinkling at the edges, a smile playing on his lips.

I shake my head, turn my page and settle into the next sketch. This time Jesse is sort of leaning across the theatre block. I am determined to do a better job.

I start again, trying to follow Betty's advice, trying to keep my eyes on Jesse as much as I can. You have to look, I tell myself, if you don't look you won't know what to draw. I do my best, trying to ignore the colour in my cheeks. I get to his dangly bits and try to quickly sketch them, continuing to the rest of his body, taking care not to make his legs, or anything else, too long.

Much better.

I stand back to assess and Oh. My. Gosh.

This. Is. Worse.

So. Much. Worse.

It takes everything I have in me not to groan out loud. I absolutely cannot draw attention to myself now. I cover my face with my hands. I feel heat radiating off my skin.

The problem this time is not so much one of length, but direction. While Jesse is lying down, it appears as if part of him is standing to attention. How? How could I have got this so, so wrong?

This absolutely must be fixed. Bare below the waist is nothing in comparison to this blunder. If I was working in pencil, I could just erase the lines. But no. It just had to be charcoal.

I peek out from behind my easel. Betty is a few students over, and she looks like she is coming this way again. Without thinking I attempt to rub the charcoal off the page with my hand. But charcoal doesn't work like that, and now I have black all over my hand and a terrible smudge on my page that now presents some sense of movement, which is quite possibly even worse. If that is even a thing.

Shit.

Betty is getting closer and she cannot see this.

I flip the page and start again.

I don't want her to ask what has happened. *Act natural, Cleo.* I smile at Betty and give her a little wave. Before realising that I'm waving the hand that is smeared black from attempting to rub the saluting soldier off the page.

Super smooth and absolutely natural.

Not.

Get it together, Cleo. You can do this.

Betty comes closer. 'Mistakes are fine. Part of the process. Remember what we are doing today. We are making a . . .' Betty pauses, looking into my eyes and waiting for me to fill in the blank.

'Mess?'

'Yes, and not just that, we are having fun doing it. Celebrate your mistakes, don't be ashamed of them. You will learn more from your mistakes than your successes. In fact, count the mistakes as successes.' Betty reaches over and flips the page with my sketch back over. 'Look here, see how well you've captured his shoulders, his neckline. Beautiful. And as to this . . . *stirring*, shall we say?' I can't help it; a giggle escapes me. 'Maybe this is all you should focus on for the next couple of images? Maybe you will create a whole series? Who knows?' Betty must see the horror in my face. 'Or maybe not, but it's just a part of his body and I'm sure you've learnt something.'

She's right, I have. I've learnt that I'm clearly way more comfortable with the female form.

I have been so focused on the mess on my page that I've forgotten who is next to me. Mattias surveys the mess on my page and hand, a nondescript look on his face. When I look up again, I see his shoulders shaking slightly and I realise his expression. The jerk is laughing at me and trying not to let me see!

Without thinking, my arm shoots out and gives him a shove. But then I realise I've touched him and I freeze awkwardly and have to literally tell myself to lower my arm and move away.

He doesn't seem to notice my weirdness, only wobbles a little, smiles more and looks down at the black smudge on his white shirt.

Serves him right.

He then looks at me, spreading his arms wide as if asking, *What did I do to deserve that?*

I refuse to answer, both because I'm not sure how and because it's a matter of principle, so I look pointedly back at Jesse.

'I think it might be time for a quick drink break,' says Betty. 'Have a drink while Jesse stretches and maybe take a look at some of the work around you. Then we'll have time for a couple more poses before we break for food.'

As soon as Betty finishes speaking, I turn back to Mattias. 'Don't laugh at me,' I tell him.

He holds his hands up again, this time in surrender. 'Sorry,' he says and when he looks back at his artwork I pull a face at him. Super mature, but somehow it makes me feel a tiny bit better.

Chapter Seven

After lunch we settle into drawing again, with a new model. Shelly. I manage to begin straight away and get through the session without embarrassing myself. I'm counting that as a win. Overall, it has been a good day, albeit with some awkward moments.

As I pack up my things Lachlan appears at my elbow.

'Hey, Cleo from Camden,' he says, and I can't help but turn to him with a smile. 'Are you catching the train home?' he asks.

I nod in reply and finish zipping up my bag. 'Yeah, sure am.'

'Me too, let's walk together. See ya, Remi, thanks again, Betty,' he says, beaming some of his light towards her. It's all I can do not to point to myself and ask, *Me? Did you mean me?* Lachlan has this way of making people feel seen, and it's nice to feel seen.

'Bye, Remi,' I say. Then, worrying that I'm excluding her, I quickly add, 'Actually, are you going to the station too?'

'Not straight away, I wanted to catch Betty anyhow. I'll see you both tomorrow.'

I love how easy Remi is to be around and I hope, not for the first time, that I will get to spend more time with her over the rest of the summer. We have four weeks of classes, three days a week – twelve classes in total – and I'm glad to have people like Remi around me.

'Thank you for the class, Betty,' I say as we walk towards the exit.

'You're welcome, lovely, you did some great work today,' she replies and I assume it's completely in my head but it's like everyone is looking at me and Lachlan as we walk together. I feel special.

Lachlan pauses before the door and gestures for me to go ahead of him.

We walk for the first twenty metres or so without talking but it's not awkward at all, it feels good to have someone with me.

'How did you find today?' I ask Lachlan.

'Yeah good, it was good,' he says, but it seems like his head is somewhere else.

‘I thought so too,’ I say, and leave it at that.

We walk a little further and I am aware of a familiar face passing us. It’s Mattias. He salutes us and keeps going, taking long, quick strides, not stopping to say anything to us. ‘See ya, soldier,’ I call out pronouncing soldier as sold-ya so that it rhymes. I immediately regret my choice of words. When have I ever said that before? Why am I so weird around him?

Lachlan groans. ‘That guy,’ he says, not noticing my embarrassment.

‘What about him?’ I ask. ‘Do you know him?’

‘Not really, I don’t know . . .’ he trails off, changing the subject, which is a relief. ‘Actually Cleo, I need you to help me out with something.’

I like when he says my name.

‘Sure,’ I say, pausing to look over at him.

‘I’ve decided I’m going to throw a party.’

‘Okay.’

‘But it’s not going to be worthwhile if you can’t come.’

‘Oh.’

‘Yeah, so you have to tell me if you are free. If I do it this Saturday, can you come?’

I am flattered. ‘Sure, um, I have work in the morning but I think I can make it. What time are you thinking?’

‘The party will start when you arrive so whenever works for you.’

Oh, you sweet boy, that is nowhere near enough detail. My face must show my uncertainty.

'Sometime after eight?'

'Sounds good,' I say, totally nailing the transition from unsure to cool.

Two things can be true at the same time. I can be excited that a boy, for reasons unbeknownst to me, has invited me to a party and actually wants me there. This is clearly not a pity invite; I am completely across what a pity invite looks like. It actually sucks. It really doesn't make anyone feel better; in fact, I think it does the opposite. The person doing the inviting clearly is only doing it because they feel some sort of outdated sense of moral obligation, or their mum has made them. And the person being invited might feel excited for a moment, but when they realise that no one actually wants them there . . . well, let's just say, it's rough. So, while feeling pumped that Lachlan, this confident, shiny boy, wants me there, I am also a bit worried. Because parties mean groups of random people and finding your way to new places and drunken idiots and sometimes the introvert in me wants to hang at home in my comfort zone and not interact with anyone. Scratch the sometimes, most times is far more accurate. But this is Lachlan, and I am well aware attending a party is on my final-year-of-school plan, so that feels fortuitous (even though I have sworn off most plans).

'Yeah, I can be there around then,' I confirm – and look at me, so easy, so breezy.

'In that case, the party will go ahead. Oh hey, let's get ice cream,' Lachlan says, pulling me into a convenience store.

One Magnum Ego and a vanilla Cornetto later and we are back on the bustling street.

'Do you ever get called Lochie?' I ask in between licks.

'I get called so many things,' Lachlan says with a grin, 'and Lochie is one of them.'

'But what do you prefer?' I ask.

'As long as you're the one calling out my name, it doesn't matter.'

Was that a sex joke?

The confidence of this boy!

I roll my eyes at him.

Lachlan laughs. 'Oh, Cleo, I'm playing. You're so innocent, it's adorable.'

He pulls on my bag strap to bring me closer to him, then loops his arm through mine. The hair on his arm is coarse and his body heat seeps into my arm. 'Kidding, Cleo. Don't worry, I'll look after you. We're going to have so much fun over these school holidays, I promise. And I'll rein it in. I'll be like a protective older brother, hand on heart.'

'Deal,' I say and laugh despite myself.

When I get home, the sun still has some bite in it and I find my dad on the driveway out the front of the house in boardies, old shirt and thongs, washing his car. Both he and the Toyota are wet and sudsy. As he notices me, he reaches for the hose.

'Want to cool down?'

He doesn't wait for me to answer. He turns the hose on, twists it to mist, then gives a quick spray up in the air. Tiny water droplets cool my skin and a sense of nostalgia settles, a blanket around my heart, rather than a punch in the gut.

I slide out of my shoes and dump my bag on a patch of dry grass, out of the way of the hose. 'Want some help?'

'Never have I said no to that question.' He points with a dripping sponge. 'Stuff's over there.'

We work without talking.

I settle into the job I most enjoy: cleaning the bugs off the front number plate and bumper. Squatting down, I get to work, pressing hard with the sponge then using my index fingernail to try to get the most stubborn ones off. It is in fact probably the shittiest part of cleaning the car, and my sister never had the patience for it. I remember the time Dad delegated this job to her; she threw the sponge in the bushes and stormed off towards the house, her gumboots making splashy squelches as she stomped. Dad chuckled at her hissy fit, earning him a silent but meaningful glare from the porch. Dad tried to contain it, but the movement of his shoulders gave him away.

'Don't you laugh at me,' she shouted, arms firmly crossed.

She liked the bigger jobs. Sweeping movement, better return for her effort. But I was happy focusing on the minutiae. While she cleaned and danced along to whatever old music Dad was playing, I scrubbed away, daydreaming about each little bug, in my own soapy little microcosm.

Dad's voice brings me back. 'Remember when we used to do this all together?'

'First Sunday afternoon of every month,' I say.

'And probably more often when there was marking to do or reports due.'

'Really?'

'What can I say? I procrastinate with the best of them.' He sighs. 'I loved doing this with you girls. You were so funny, so different,' he says, and I let him savour the memory just as I have been doing.

'Why did we stop?' I ask.

'Your lives just got busier and busier. You were swimming and doing schoolwork or working on your projects. And Emmy was, well, you know what she was like, always had something happening, someone to see, or something to do.' He pauses, caught in the past. 'Time with parents loses its shine as you get older.' He wipes his face, and I can't be sure if it's a tear or a soapy splash he's getting rid of. 'That's the sad irony of it; we want more of your time and you have less to give. We teach you, train you so you can be independent, but really, we are trying to prepare ourselves and the truth of it is, we'll never be ready to let you go.' He gives me a sad little smile. 'Sorry, darling, who would have thought washing the car together would make me so philosophical.'

I laugh, because amongst other subjects, philosophy is one of his favourites to teach. 'Me, Dad. It doesn't take much for you to start talking about philosophy. Isn't it always, Plato this, deontology that, moral relativism, yadda yadda?'

'Oh, happy days! I knew you were secretly listening to me,' says Dad, and he squirts me with the hose.

Chapter Eight

Day three of drawing classes and I am feeling good. My navigation has improved and I don't need my phone out to tell me where to go. I have tackled saggy boobs and wonky pensises and am prepared for whatever Betty has for us.

In the lead-up to something new, the nerves kill me. They swirl and overtake my other senses. But when I am there, when I have experienced something and can predict what will happen, I'm fine.

I am perfectly on time today and Betty bustles in with a middle-aged man who takes his place in the centre of the room. I scan the room for Lachlan but he hasn't arrived yet, so I move over to take my place next to Remi, before realising that Mattias is at the easel next to mine.

'Hi,' I whisper to Remi and I'm surprised when Mattias looks up and nods at me too.

'How're you?' Remi asks, but before we can talk any more, Betty calls the class to attention.

'Welcome to our final day for the week,' says Betty. 'We will try something different again this morning because I don't want you to feel too comfortable just yet. You've probably started to get used to your spot in the room. You might feel like an easel is yours. But I don't want you to get stuck there and I want you to know that you can move if you want to, and it's good to get a new perspective. So today we are going to be a little more active in our work. More collaborative. It's a bit out there, I know. Other teachers might question the merit of the activity. However, in the interest of trying new things, of shaking it up, of getting a little bit messy' – my three least favourite things – 'we are going to give this a go.' Betty notices Lachlan at the door and ushers him in. 'Today you will be drawing Clayton.' From the centre of the room, Clayton gives a nod. 'However, the artwork won't just be your own. So, with that in mind, let's begin, using a pencil.'

I start with Clayton's arm. His elbow, pointed up, makes the highest point in my artwork. I work down to his shoulder and am working on sketching his head when Betty says, 'Freeze!'

It's funny how conditioned we are. Our collective childhood memory of party games kicks into gear and all of us turn to statues, different expressions frozen across our faces. Mine is momentary panic, and out of the corner of my eye I see Mattias's bemused grin spread across his handsome face.

'Well done,' Betty says, and I can tell she enjoys the power of this moment. 'Now if everyone can move to the easel on their right. That's it, everyone moving in a circle.' She points to Imogen. 'Yes, all the way across, that's it. You should now be standing in front of your neighbour's easel. They may not have done as much as you, or they may have done more. Their approach may be different. That's a good thing. We are now building on their work. It will feel strange; it might look strange, but keep working. You may fill their work in, but never erase it – always continue it. Now begin.'

'Let's go.' I can hear Lachlan across the room.

'Loving this energy, thank you, Lachlan,' Betty says.

I look over to him and he throws me a shaka. Totally Lachlan.

Next to me, Remi begins. 'I'll do my best,' I whisper to her.

'Make your best mess!' she whispers back, giving me permission to go for it.

Remi's angle is ever so slightly different from mine, and while I've been drawing lines, getting the shape, Remi has begun shading as she goes. Looking up at Clayton and then only briefly back at the page, I try to mimic Remi's style. I'm not nailing it, but I also don't feel like I've ruined the drawing. I'm wondering if anyone beside Remi and myself could tell where her drawing ends and mine begins.

I sneak a look at Mattias next to me. He is intensely focused. I'm not sure why but it bothers me. Like he's more serious about it than I was, which is weird. I feel an urge to break his concentration. I raise my eyebrows at him.

'Freeze!' says Betty. I do not freeze with my eyebrows up. For more than a second.

'Move to your right again and finish the sketch off.'

We do as Betty says. We stop and step back, then move together in a circle. It's like speed dating, but with artwork. I reassess the page in front of me now. It's slightly different again. I look at Clayton, my perspective shifting, my line of sight new. This artwork belonged to Amina, then Remi and now it is mine too. I continue the work, but I can see Mattias in my peripheral vision. He is still in serious mode, his face fixed in a frown. It makes me feel like I've done a terrible job and now he has had to come along and fix it. Which is exactly what Betty said was NOT the point of the exercise.

'Is it that bad?' I want to ask him, but I can't work up the courage. I know as soon as I open my mouth around him something stupid will come out.

Instead I take to sneaking looks at him, hoping that he might start enjoying himself and stop hating my artwork. But he doesn't start to look happier and he doesn't seem to notice my preoccupation with his mood.

'Freeze,' says Betty. 'I know you want to move to your right, you creatures of habit, but let's really shake it up. Move across the room to any other easel.'

No one moves.

'Any easel, let's go, try diagonal, across the circle, doesn't matter where, just long as you don't stay at the same place,' she points Kiaan towards a free easel as the rest of us shuffle across the semicircle. 'Now let's begin a new piece. One minute!'

Despite having crossed the circle, Mattias is still next to me, his hyperfocus continuing to distract me. I wonder why I'm so bothered by it. At least it's not my work he's frowning at now, and if he's focused, I should be too. I shouldn't be worrying about what he's doing. It's completely irrational. But who am I if not irrational?

I look up at Clayton again, trying to regain focus. Betty is right, I was used to being on the other side of the room. Being this side is odd. I take a look at the sketch Mattias has started on to see how much his angle has changed, then steal a glance back at him. When he looks up, perhaps feeling me gaze, I quickly turn my head back towards my work and pretend it's what I have been doing all along.

After a moment, I sneak another look back at him. His eyes meet mine, catching me out.

I gasp in surprise.

A loud intake of breath.

I attempt to cover it with a cough.

Mattias raises his eyebrows at me, so I go all in and cough some more to distract him from what actually happened.

I finish with a little, and what I would call dignified, clearing of my throat, when I hear someone say, 'My brother sounds just like that when he is having an asthma attack.'

'Does *she* have asthma?' someone else asks from a few places over.

'What?' I splutter, the surprise of the question turning my fake cough to a real one, my face betraying me as the familiar feel of heat floods my cheeks.

'I don't think so,' Betty muses, walking over to the desk at the front of the room and opening her laptop. 'But someone did have asthma in here, or was that a peanut allergy? I better check.'

'I'm fine,' I manage, but I'm sure I don't look it.

From the middle of the room, Clayton, arms fixed in place, head completely still, slides to his left slightly and manages to kick his bag in my direction. 'There's an inhaler in there, love. Front pocket, next to the glasses. Asthma's not something to be trifled with.'

I look back at him, encouraged by the care he's shown but unsure how to precede.

By now everyone has abandoned their work and is looking at me.

Clayton nods in my direction again. 'Go on.'

I 100 per cent regret my commitment to coughing.

Do I reach for Clayton's bag and get the inhaler?

Do I fess up?

How did things escalate that quickly?

Clayton remains in his pose in the middle of the room, completely still . . . apart from his eyes, which move from his bag to me, silently imploring me to take the inhaler.

I am about to succumb to peer pressure and reach for the bag when Betty slams her laptop closed. 'Nope, no asthmatics here, and it was wasp stings not peanut butter.'

'I'll just have a sip of water,' I say, mortified.

I silently vow never to look at or talk to Mattias again.

When the day ends, Lachlan steps up next to Betty. 'Hey, everyone,' he says. You can tell he likes being the centre of attention and how comfortable he is. 'First of all, what a great week we've been having, I'm sure I'm not alone in my gratitude for this workshop. I'm looking forward to the rest of our time here together. Also, I know some of you will have exchanged numbers already, but I'd love to get a group chat going. You never know when it'll come in handy. I'm going to set up it up, so don't go till I've got your number!' He smiles at everyone and I'm struck again by his ease with people. So different to Mattias. Lachlan holds his hands up. 'So hey, also, full disclosure, I do have a vested interest in doing this. I'm having a party, on Saturday. It's late notice, but come anyway.' He looks at me, pauses and winks. 'I'll send the deets out in the chat. Don't go till I've got your number!'

While Lachlan circles the room, I make a beeline towards Remi. 'Are you doing anything this weekend?'

'I might be looking after my brother,' says Remi, 'and I'm out Sunday morning, but nothing much.'

'So, do you think you'll come? Go? To the party, I mean.'

'You're going to go?'

'Yeah, Lachlan was talking about it earlier. I'm planning to go. Please come. It'd be way better if you are there. It'd be fun to hang out some more, outside of here, I mean.' I don't want to sound like I'm begging her.

'I think I can make it work,' says Remi. 'What about you, Mattias?' She turns to him across the circle, including him in the conversation. 'Will you come too?'

He looks at me before speaking, as if I hold his answer. I clearly do not.

'I'll see,' he says, and I can tell that's a no. Quite frankly, it feels like a relief.

Plan For Going to Parties

For Cleo Markson by Emmaline Markson

1. *Choose your outfit carefully. Don't just pick something based on what it looks like or what it feels like, but choose something by how it makes you feel. Do you need to feel powerful? Relaxed? Comfortable? Hot? (Not temperature wise) Warm? (Temperature wise) Interesting? Choose something that will give you the right feels.*
2. *Don't be early, that's awkward. Unless you've planned ahead to help them set up. Come at least twenty minutes after the start time, more if it's not a food party – they mostly aren't.*
3. *If you can't find anyone to talk to, give yourself a mission. You could go to get some food, or drink, or go to the toilet. Something that makes you feel like you have a purpose. Having a purpose will give you confidence.*
4. *If you feel weird and you don't know what to do with your hands, hold something, like a drink.*
5. *But, if you want to drink, make sure you eat too. Also, for every drink, try to have two cups of water.*
6. *And always know how you are getting home.*
7. *If you want to talk to someone but don't know what to say, go with something like, 'So how do you know the host?' Then refer to the Plan for Conversations.*
8. *Have fun!*

Chapter Nine

'Just be safe,' my mum tells me as I unbuckle my seatbelt. 'And feel free to call me at any time; I'll stay in the area. I'm going to visit an old friend.' She stares at me until I turn and catch her eye. 'Call me any time,' she says again, maintaining eye contact until I nod in agreement.

'Mum, yes, we've been through this.' I've got to get out of the car. 'I promise to be sensible. I know all about drink spiking and condoms and not accepting pills from strangers until I know their exact chemical make-up and not diving into pools from balconies.' I'm trying to be light, because I'm clearly not going to be taking any pills, regardless of their make-up, and I don't even know if Lachlan has a pool. But my list of dangerous behaviours seems to spook Mum and now I don't know quite where to go with it. 'I'll be fine,' I say.

I jump out of Mum's car before I have to apologise, slam the door shut and then head towards Lachlan's front entrance. I always got rich-kid vibes from him and one look at this place confirms it. The front lawn is sprawling and there is a full turning circle out the front of the property. The house is a modern beauty, full of angles and light, and I can't quite imagine what growing up in there would have been like.

Noise pulsates through the windows. I can hear the loud chatter of a throng of people and I am almost wishing for the comfort of our Toyota's rear seat.

I'm not sure what the protocol here is. Do I knock on the door? Ring the bell? That seems a tad too formal. So, do I just walk in? This is the bit I hate. My hesitation is rewarded by the slap of slides on gravel and I turn to see a group of three girls whose level of personal grooming I couldn't hope to attain.

'Friend of Lochie's?' the blonde one asks. She looks vaguely familiar and as she comes closer, I realise where I've seen her before. Lachlan's feed. It's @sunnydaze2230. Her love for warm weather stands in contrast to the icy chill she projects towards me.

I swallow my nerves and adopt a fake-it-till-you-make-it smile. 'Yep, just about to head in.'

She gives me a once-over, her eyes flicking from my slightly rusted Birks that my sister passed on to me, up to the top of my jeans, white tank and messy bun. 'So how do you know Lochie?' she asks. And it's not the fact that she asks, because that makes sense (it's a great conversation starter, I've used it myself), it's how she does it that makes my toes curl. Like she's not just asking one question but two. It's her *tone*. The way she says it adds so much more meaning. So, while she is asking me *how* I know him it feels like she actually wants to know *why*. Like she is questioning my ability to exist in the same realm as Lachlan.

I give her a tight smile. One that doesn't reach my eyes or show my teeth. 'We just met, actually, in the city.' The tone I'm aiming for is light and breezy, confident, but also a little obtuse. Let her wonder.

She looks me over again. 'It's the art thing, isn't it?'

Damn. I've lost my mysterious angle.

'Yeah, we're in the same class. Drawing doodles together.'

Silence.

I can hear her friend's intake of breath.

And now I'm not only not mysterious, but I also sound like a deranged toddler. The familiar sensation of a full-blown flushed face hits me and I turn back to the door. Suddenly, walking right in feels like the best option.

'Let's go, shall we?' I don't wait for her answer. I push open the oversized front door before I can embarrass myself even further. *Drawing doodles*? Who says that?

My cheeks are definitely red now and the last thing I want to do is walk into a room filled with strangers but turning back around is even less of an option.

I can hear the girls behind me and I tell my feet to go forwards.

I move through what I think can only be described as a foyer, which is as big as my lounge room. There are a handful of people hanging out here but none of them looks even vaguely familiar, so I push on towards where I think the kitchen could be. I'm hoping the girls will peel off from behind me at some point but I force myself not to turn to check.

The kitchen is full of people and I head for the marbled benchtop. It's good to have a purpose in this sort of situation. My purpose is to find something to put in my hands so perhaps I will look like I belong, even if I don't feel like it. I find some plastic cups at one end of the sink.

'Excuse me, sorry,' I say as I navigate past a group of thick-necked boys. The are all similar size to Lachlan, their shoulders wide. My presence is not acknowledged.

'It was clearly LBW,' says one.

'Nah, mate, too high,' says the other.

'And you're four for twenty-two, take the win.'

There is an assortment of different soft drinks sitting on the bench and as I pour myself something fizzy with the promise of lemon and lime, I'm not sure whether I want someone to talk to me or not.

Also scattered on the bench are bowls of chips and some slightly sad-looking party pies. I'm considering the merit of a cold pie when I hear a welcome voice. 'Cleo from Camden, you made it! Welcome to my hood! Have you met the boys? We've got Harry, Cooper and Archie.' He points in the direction of each of the boys as he says their names. 'What a game today, boys! Cleo, can you believe Archie came away with four for twenty-two?'

If I knew what that meant I might find it hard to believe, but do I care? Lachlan wraps an arm around my shoulders, giving me a squeeze. Maybe I could? Maybe I do?

'Yeah, um, well done,' I manage, hoping the four for twenty-two is something to be happy about.

'Cleo's in my art class; we're having all kinds of fun together.' He winks at me, like we have an inside joke. 'Fellas, I'll catch you in a bit, I'm going to show Cleo around.' I love how easy Lachlan is around people. Like nothing phases him. Lachlan's breath is warm on my face and I can smell a hint of beer on his breath. I'm so relieved he has found me. 'Let's go Cle-oh,' Lachlan cheers as he steers me away from the bench and into the living room. 'Did it take you long to get here?'

'Not too long, it's closer than the city.'

'Nice. So, what are we going to get up to tonight? Will we follow Betty's advice?'

'How do you mean?' I ask.

'Should we get a little messy?'

I'm still not entirely sure what he means by that, until he shepherds me to a buffet against the wall and takes out a half-empty glass bottle of clear liquid with a red label and lid. Betty's words stick in my ears and I think, you know what? Maybe I can be a go-with-the-flow Cleo. Maybe getting messy is just what I need.

'Is that your plan, Lochie?' I ask.

Lachlan turns his body to face mine. 'You know I'm not into making plans,' he says.

'Me neither,' I say unsure of whether this is the truth or not.

I hold out my cup.

'Okay,' I say. 'Betty's way. Let's do it.'

Lachlan tops it up with the vodka from the bottle.

'To naked bodies,' he says conspiratorially.

'And to drawing them.' We knock our cups together and drink. I take a small sip. It's not awful. I take another.

'Is Remi coming tonight?' I ask. 'I thought she'd be here by now.'

'You didn't see the group text? She had to bail. Her mum got held up and needed her at home with her brother.'

I pull my phone out of my back pocket. I can't believe I missed her message. If I had known I wouldn't have come. I really only know Lachlan.

'Don't stress, Cleo. I'm glad you're here. That's why I came to find you. You want to dance? Come on, let's pick some tunes.'

I am so relieved to have Lachlan next to me. So relieved not to be in this room of people all by myself.

'What you do you think, Cleo, classic hits or fresh bangers? You strike me as more of a classic hits kind of girl.' I don't know what he means by that. 'Shall we have a 90s playlist?'

I'm not sure I want to dance, much less what my music choice is, but as soon as I hear Scary Spice sing out the first few words of 'Wannabe' and see Lachlan wiggling his shoulders, I decide that I don't need to be sure. I just need to be. I finish my drink in one go and allow Lachlan to lead me to dance floor, aka the lounge room, where someone has pushed the cream leather lounges back to make room. As Spice Girls leads to TLC which leads to what feels like a beer anthem about getting knocked down, I let myself go. I don't care if we are dancing to this music in an ironic or unironic way. I don't care that

I don't know anyone else here and that Remi didn't come. I don't care that my sister would disapprove of my lack of water intake. I don't care that Lachlan's friends don't give a rat's arse about me; I am getting messy and I feel free. My heart pulses in time to the beat and I shimmy my shoulders and swing my hips in time to the music. Normally I am the person at the edge of the dance floor worried that everyone is looking at her. But not tonight.

When 'Pony' comes on, Lachlan leans in. His lips move but I can't make out his words. I think he senses my confusion because he leans further in. For a split second my breath catches and I wonder if he is going to kiss me, but his cheek lightly brushes mine as he speaks directly into my ear.

'I'm getting another drink, you want one?'

I meet his eyes and nod. 'Yes.'

The tunes keep coming and I know if Emmy was here, she would be shaking her head at me and laughing at the same time.

After three more songs my mouth is feeling dry and I wonder where Lachlan has gotten to. I push my way out of the gyrating bodies towards the kitchen. I see Lachlan standing in the corner and am about to go to him when I'm given reason to pause. Lachlan is speaking to @sunnydaze2230 and while I am not a body-language expert, I can tell she is not happy. There is a tension hanging in the air like thick smog and I don't know what my next move should be.

I feel an internal tug of war. I want to hear more but at the same time I know this is not a conversation meant for me. Lachlan's back is facing towards me and sunnydaze is gesticulating wildly. Maybe if I just grab a drink? I take two steps closer to the bench but freeze when sunnydaze pauses her tirade mid-sentence to look at me. I'm pretty sure that if eyes could shoot daggers, I would need a whole lot more than first aid. On the upside, someone would come with a stretcher and carry me out of this uncomfortable situation.

As Lachlan turns, I skittishly reach out for the nearest drink. I mumble something along the lines of, 'Just getting a drink,' then retreat before he can say anything.

The good thing is I actually really need a drink. The bad thing is I now have a can of VB in my hand and I'm not really sure I can make myself drink it. But my gosh, I have to get out the kitchen. Now.

I turn and walk away from the room.

That was awkward. Getting messy might work in art class but it sure as hell isn't a good strategy for real life. The dance floor is still pumping as I walk past it but the joy and freedom I felt before has passed and there is no way I'm joining back in.

I reach for my phone. And start to text.

Mum, I think I might want to come home. I'll be ready when you are.

I step forward and look up all in one motion and slam right into an armpit. Luckily, my VB can remains unopened in my hand. Unluckily, a cup of Coke is not so easily contained. My right arm is dripping and when I look down, I can see a large wet patch on my shirt. I lift the material off my skin and shake the sticky liquid off my arm.

'What the –'

'Oh crap. Shoot, I'm sorry.'

'Hell yeah you should be,' I say.

'I know, that's why I apologised. But you, with your phone? You are a bit to blame.'

That's when I look up from my sodden tank top.

It's Mattias.

'You,' I say.

'Me,' he says.

Then passes me a handkerchief.

'What are you, like, ninety years old?' I ask.

'You don't have to use it.'

'Yeah, well,' I grumble, before dabbing my arm with the small white cloth. 'I want to use it.' I wipe some more before adding, 'I didn't know you were coming.'

'Lachlan invited everyone.'

'But most people didn't come.'

'No, I guess not . . . someone said something about an art show? I think that's what I heard.'

'Oh.'

He shrugs. 'Anyway, I was invited so here I am.'

'But you don't really socialise.'

'Well, that's not quite true.' He pauses, then adds, 'And also a little harsh.'

'But fair,' I say.

'What makes you say I don't socialise?'

Does he really want me to answer this? He seems to be waiting for my answer.

'Maybe the fact that you don't really hang out with anyone at the class. You seem to disappear off to have your lunch by yourself. You literally can't have a conversation and you either laugh at people's artwork, or you frown at it. Also, the fact that the very first time when I was about to introduce myself you couldn't get away fast enough.' I thought I was over that. Obviously, I'm not. And it seems the vodka has loosened my tongue. 'Plus, and I could be wrong, but this feels like the most anyone from class has ever spoken to you. Can you think of any other conversation you've had that has gone for longer than this one?'

He seems to consider it for a moment. 'I chatted to my mum before I left home,' he says.

'You've just proved my point.'

He shrugs. 'Maybe so. Well, that's not true, we've talked before.'

'I'm not sure I'd define any of our interactions as proper conversations.' They've either been one-sided monologues about my dad calling the roll or terrible misunderstandings ending in resounding embarrassment.

He laughs. At me.

My phone dings. It's my mum.

I'll be about 20 mins.

'That's my lift,' I say. 'You'll have to find someone else to have an awkward interaction with, because I'm going.'

It's a good way to exit. He doesn't need to know Mum is still on her way. At this point I'd definitely prefer to wait outside by myself than have a one-sided conversation with this arrogant jerk who has just spilled drink all over me. I can take the time to pull myself together. I walk towards the front door. I figure I can message Lachlan and thank him for inviting me and let him know I've gone home. I definitely don't want to get in the middle of whatever was going on with him and sunnydaze.

I make my way towards the front door, open it, step through and wait for it to click shut behind me. But it doesn't. Because someone else comes out after me.

Chapter Ten

It's Mattias. Again.

What I really want is to ignore him. It's what feels best for everyone. I step towards the balcony railing and lean on it. Even though it's a warm night, there is a gentle breeze that licks at my arms. The cool of the railing sinks into my skin. The fabric of my top sits cold and wet on my chest. I shiver.

Out of the corner of my eye I see Mattias start unbuttoning his olive-green linen shirt. It's too much.

'What are you doing?' I explode.

'I'm about to pose for you,' he says, raising one hand to his ear and resting the other on his hip. There is no hint of sarcasm in his voice and quite frankly I just don't get him. I don't know where I stand with him so I'm unsure how to respond. My face is blank.

'I'm joking,' he clarifies. 'You look cold and wet and I'm sort of to blame for that.' His shirt is off now. He hands it to me. 'Consider it a peace offering. Plus, I'm wearing two.' Under his shirt is a navy tee.

'So, you are a grandpa,' I say, even though it's not a singlet he has on underneath.

'Do you want the shirt or not?'

The shirt is still warm from his body and as he passes it to me his fingers brush mine, surprising me and making me pull back. His shirt smells like he does: fresh, a little like the ocean, really good. Which somehow annoys me even more. I grimace.

'Are you smelling my shirt?'

'It's possible.'

The corners of his mouth turn upwards. So obnoxious.

'Does it smell bad?'

I know it's petty but I don't answer. Instead, I say, 'You'll have to turn around.' I motion to my wet top.

As he turns, I wiggle my arms out, slide them into his shirt, buttoning it up before sliding my wet top down my body and stepping out of it. While he's not looking, I take one final smell of the shirt before I tuck it in loosely at the front and hang my wet top over the rail so I don't have to hold it while I wait. 'Done.'

He turns around, meeting my eyes. 'Good.'

'Thanks.'

We are both silent.

'So, what do –'

'Is this a –'

We speak at the same time.

We both stop. This conversation is so awkward. Talking to him is impossible.

He motions for me to continue.

'Is this a normal Saturday night for you?'

'No. You?'

'No.' My answer comes out stronger than I intended it to.

'Really? You looked like you were having a great time in there.'

'Is that an accusation?' I sound snarkier than I mean to, but he makes me feel so uncertain.

'You were dancing.'

'You saw me dancing?' This conversation is verging into weird territory again and maybe I wasn't snarky enough.

He shrugs. 'Sure.'

'You were watching me dance?'

'No! I mean I saw you dancing but not in some creepy, I-was-sitting-in-the-corner-watching-you way. I just saw you dancing when I got here.'

I'm not sure how, but he still manages to sound judgemental.

'Right,' I say. 'I think it's better when we don't talk.'

In the silence, Mattias moves so that he is also leaning on the railing, about one metre away from me. I know parties aren't my usual Saturday night entertainment. I know that *I* came because I thought Remi was going to be here and because I thought it could be fun to hang out with Lachlan. And it *was* fun, while it lasted. But what I can't work out is why Mattias is here. He doesn't even seem to like the people in the class, so why would he come to a party to hang out with them? I mean, it was a universal invitation; Lachlan wouldn't care if people came or not.

I turn to Mattias and break the silence. 'So, sorry, I still don't understand, why are you here again?'

'I came to give you my shirt.'

'No, not out on the balcony with me. I mean, that is also a good question, but why are you at the party?' Mattias shrugs, so I continue with my line of questioning. 'Because as previously stated, you don't seem to like us and you just said you don't really go to parties. So why' – I wave my arms around for emphasis – 'are you here?'

Mattias goes to start but I cut him off again. 'And don't give me any invitation bull because I think we both know that's not true.'

I keep my eyes on his until he looks away.

'Did Lachlan say we've met before?' Mattias flicks his hair out of his face before continuing. 'We went to the same high school for about a term, in year 7.'

'You went to that sports school?'

'No. He was at my school.'

'Huh.' I try to remember if Lachlan has said anything like that. I'm drawing a blank. 'He never mentioned that. In fact, I think he said he didn't know you.'

'I don't think he remembers me.'

'Why don't you just talk to him in class?'

'I haven't really had the chance.'

'So why aren't you inside talking to Lachlan now?'

'He's been fairly occupied since I got here, and I thought I could be of use here.'

He's got me on that one. Lachlan's either been with me or with sunnydaze. And as much as I don't want to admit it, I am thankful for the loan of the shirt.

I give in. 'I appreciate the shirt,' I say, and he nods, accepting the thanks.

We both fall into silence. It's neither comfortable nor uncomfortable. But then it continues and no one says anything and the longer it goes on the more unbearable it feels.

The words of some song I've not heard before filters out.

'Do you like this song?' I ask to break the silence between us.

'No.'

I wait for him to ask me if I like it.

He doesn't.

'You're not going to ask if I like it?'

'Well, I wasn't.'

'You're not a great conversationalist, are you?'

'So, you've told me.'

'Because it's true, you're not exactly easy to talk to. Normally, I would ask a question, then you would answer and ask me one back, it's kind of how conversation works.' I know I'm being snarky again but there is something about this boy that puts me off balance and it's like I forget how to be a normal person around him and my default is either rambling awkwardness, ridiculous behaviour resulting in utter embarrassment or, and this a new one from tonight, just telling him off. At this point I'm definitely enjoying telling him off more than the other options. I feel weirdly powerful.

Mattias shrugs and smiles. 'Well, you said it was better that we didn't talk.'

He is infuriating.

'You know, *some* people are friendly, you can have a chat with them without feeling like they are silently judging you for your dancing, which by the way *was* a lot of fun. *Some* people make you feel comfortable and welcome.' Was that too far? Is my tongue way too loose? Am I just a really mean drunk?

'Some people, hey?'

'Yes, some people.' I don't care if I'm making him feel bad.

'Some people like Lachlan?' I think I detect a slight eye roll as he says this.

'Well, if you want to put a name to it, I guess so.'

'So, what you're saying is, I'm not Lachlan?'

'I didn't say that.'

'But that's what you were implying.'

'Maybe. Fine, yes. Lachlan *is* easy to talk to. I know where I stand with Lachlan. He makes people feel comfortable and accepted.'

'Well, I'm so glad he makes *you* feel comfortable.' Mattias's voice is laced with some sort of emotion that I can't quite identify and again I'm not sure where this conversation is going or why it's going. He is still not looking at me. I take the opportunity to stare at his face. His brow is creased and his lips are pulled into a grimace. I absolutely cannot understand him. I want to ask him why he's reacted like that but I'm pretty sure he won't tell me.

I try to shrug the whole conversation off. It now feels like I've pushed too far, been too rude and I am starting to regret it. 'Anyway, I guess we're all good at different things,' I say.

Mattias is silent for a moment then turns to face me, holding eye contact. 'What do you think you're good at, Cleo?'

I asked for a question and he's given it to me, that's for sure. I don't really know how to answer this one. I feel my frustration continuing to thaw as I think about his question.

'We-ellllllllllll . . .' I draw the word out into two syllables, attempting to buy some more time. I can easily tell him all the things my sister was good at. Good at taking risks, incredible at netball, brilliant at telling stories that made you feel like you had been there. But what am I good at? I'm not good in new situations. I'm no good in a crisis. Making decisions sends me into a frenzy. I'm terrible at netball. The umpire was constantly blowing the whistle at me, calling, 'Travel!' when I had the ball; it got to be that my team mates just wouldn't throw the ball to me no matter how open I was. I used to think I was okay at drawing, but looking at other people's work has convinced me that I'm really not great.

Mattias raises his eyebrows, his green eyes searching mine, waiting for an answer.

'I thought I was getting better at making new friends but clearly I'm mistaken,' I say, gesturing to him and myself, as a way of saying, *Clearly, I haven't done very well here.*

Mattias shakes his head. 'That's not a proper answer. What are you good at?'

I feel like I've lost all control of this conversation. Normally good conversation goes back and forth, it's balanced, no one has the upper hand. But after the whole shirt thing, I was leading the conversation, and now it feels like I'm being dared to keep up. I've accused Mattias of being bad at conversation, but if I can't answer this question then that falls back on me. It's the rules of conversation. Which makes me think of my sister again, which gives me an idea. 'I think I'm good at being a little sister,' I say.

Mattias nods. 'Okay, but what does that mean?'

'Are you my therapist now?'

'If I was, what would you say?'

As he asks, there is a shout from inside and three of the cricket guys tumble out. One shouts, 'On your marks, get set, go!' and fumbles with his phone.

The other two leap the front steps and set off at quite a pace down Lachlan's drive, pushing each other away and trying to get ahead. The one with the phone (Archie maybe, or was it Cooper?) shrugs, takes a mouthful of beer and turns to go back inside.

'I think I would want to know why a therapist was at a teenage party with more than a little bit of underage drinking.'

'And that would be a valid question. Thankfully I'm not your therapist.'

'Why thankfully? Do I have too many issues? Would you always feel I was your one patient that you couldn't help?'

'Stop trying to shift the focus! That's not what I mean.

What makes someone a good little sister? It's a serious question; I'm an only child so I am interested in your answer.'

I sigh. 'I guess . . .' I trail off again, trying to rearrange my thoughts and work out what I want to say. I look out at the front lawn rather than facing Mattias. 'So, here's the thing: I'm actually terrible at a lot of stuff, like making decisions and feeling comfortable in new settings. But my sister always felt so good at everything I was bad at. And that was okay. Because instead of making me feel terrible about how much better she was, she would help me, you know?'

I turn to face Mattias, but he doesn't say anything so I continue. 'She would write me plans, sort of how-to guides, sets of rules, and I guess teach me different things. I always felt like she had my back. That she would always be there to help me.'

After a beat Mattias looks towards me. 'You know you've just managed to tell me the things you're bad at again? You told me what your sister did that was great but not about yourself.'

Damn it, he's right. But I can't admit it. 'Okay, no, it's there. So, what makes me a good little sister is that I'd listen. Right? I'm good at taking her advice and learning from it. And I wouldn't get upset because she had things I didn't have or because she was better at things than I was, like most little sisters, because I knew she'd always be there to teach me. See! Hah! Point proved, that's what I'm good at!'

I have managed to answer his question but somehow I don't feel better. My feelings are a snow globe left to settle on a shelf, and some snotty kid has just come along and shaken them all up and now they are swirling around like crazy, waiting to see where they will land. I don't look back at Mattias.

'I wasn't really expecting my night to go like this,' I say in an attempt to lighten the mood. 'I didn't have any expectations, but I really didn't think this would be what I was doing.'

'Discussing your strengths and weakness on the balcony?'

'Wearing some random boy's shirt.'

'You know, for what it's worth, I think being a good listener is underrated.' Mattias bumps my foot with his and I'm surprised how the contact makes me feel.

I turn to face him. 'Thanks,' I say.

'She sounds like a great big sister.'

'Yeah.' I still don't turn to look at Mattias. My answer hangs in the air between us and I don't say any more because I don't want to see the look of sympathy that will inevitably coat his face when he realises the truth.

Luckily for me I see my mum's car pull into the driveway entrance. I grab my damp shirt from the edge of the balcony. 'That's my ride, see you at the next class. And maybe you can tell me what you're good at next time?'

'How long do you have?' Mattias asks, a smile playing on his face. 'Because it might take a while.' It seems out of character for him to say. I would expect Lachlan to say it, not Mattias. What he says next tells me he is joking. 'I'll write you a list, starting with my obvious absurd ability to follow the natural rules of a conversation and make people feel comfortable and not at all judged.'

I reach out and playfully push his shoulder and realise it's the second time I've done that to him. It's not something that I would normally do and yet I somehow have this impulse to touch him. I can't help but smile as I walk down the drive to Mum's car.

'Darling, you're looking happier than expected,' Mum says, eyeing me up and down as I open the door and slide in. She puts the car into reverse, then slams her foot on the brake when two boys stumble behind the car, yelling something about batting averages.

Chapter Eleven

On Monday, I don't get to speak to Remi before class starts and at lunch it's difficult to debrief with Lachlan there too.

'I'm so sorry I couldn't come,' says Remi. 'I felt really bad. Did you have a good time?'

'It was . . .' I think for a moment before settling on my answer '. . . fun.'

'You sound surprised,' says Remi. 'I hope Lachlan looked after you.'

'We had a great time dancing,' says Lachlan, 'but you left without saying goodbye.'

I hadn't realised he'd noticed. 'You seemed a little caught up,' I say. 'And I got chatting to someone else.'

'Yeah, okay good, I'm glad people were friendly.' He doesn't ask who it was and the conversation moves on before I can tell him it was Mattias, who hasn't said a word to me today, despite working next to me. I begin to wonder if the conversation at the party was a one-off.

After lunch, Betty looks frazzled.

'Hey, does Betty seem . . .' I trail off.

'Yeah, something's up,' agrees Remi.

'Well done everyone on making it this far. I'm so glad we haven't lost anyone. You've done more than a week's worth of the program. Your first week of life drawing class can be somewhat intimidating, so I'm glad you're all still here. But I have to say that this afternoon I've had some bad news.'

My heart sinks. I immediately lock eyes with Remi. My brain is whirling with questions. Is she going to have to cancel class? Has there been a covid outbreak? Is she going to start voting us off one by one, like an art *Survivor*? *You can't draw noses, you're out*, kind of thing?

I'm not really sure why I think Remi will have the answers. She shrugs.

'Our model has cancelled last-minute. She's quite ill. And while she was very apologetic, she has left us in a bit of a pickle.'

Next to me, Lachlan calls out, 'I can help you, Betty.'

There is laughter around the room and I feel my cheeks warm at an alarming rate. Betty doesn't skip a beat. 'Why thank you, Lachlan. I appreciate your offer. And yes, I think I'll take you up on it.'

My alarm must be written all over my face, because Betty looks directly at me and winks. 'In fact, we must all be models today.' If my cheeks were pink before, they have now transitioned to a deep beetroot. Betty pauses, enjoying the suspense, before popping the tension that has built in the room with her next words. 'You will each be modelling your hands.'

The room collectively relaxes. 'You are all familiar with your own hands and feet and I was pleased with the work you did previously. Now, you will work in pairs, studying the details of your partner's hands and recording them with your own sketches. Okay, two, two, two, two.' She partners people off around the room, putting neighbours in groups together. Lachlan and Remi are together.

'Next time, Cleo from Camden,' Lachlan says to me with a regretful smile, before turning to face Remi.

And I am left to work with Mattias. I glance sideways but he is rummaging around in his bag.

'Right . . .' says Mattias.

'I guess we'll get started then?' I ask.

'Yeah, how do you want to do this?'

I'm honestly not sure. I look around the room for inspiration. Pairs are beginning to move and configure themselves and I feel like everyone is getting on with it except for us. 'So maybe, if we turn the easels so they are facing each other?' I'm thinking aloud. 'Then kinda hold your hand out? Hmm, maybe not. What if we sit? Or we could get another stool?' Mattias gets another stool. 'We can rest our hands on that? Then we can just draw?' Everything I say is a question. This is why I hate group work. I never want to direct the action. Nothing I suggest ever feels right.

Mattias doesn't seem to mind. 'Alright, let's give it a go.'

We sit and start to draw and after about two minutes I realise this isn't going to work. I'm trying to reach my hand out around my easel but then because I'm sitting on my stool, I feel like I'm about to topple and I'm not close enough to capture the detail I was able to work on when I drew my own hand.

I can see Remi laughing as Lachlan makes different hand signals each time she looks away, then quickly relaxes his hand back when she looks again. She pulls a face at him. They look like they are having fun. My chest squeezes because a part of me wishes I was partnered with Lachlan. It's so easy to be around him.

I peek out from behind my easel to look at Mattias. He is still sketching. After a moment his head appears as he assesses my hand to continue with his work. He double-takes when he sees me staring at him.

'It's not working,' I say.

He nods in agreement. 'Cleo, how about I shift around back next to you?'

I move myself back and he re-positions himself.

'Now I guess if we shuffle closer? And then . . .' He waits till we are sitting side by side again. But I know it won't work.

'I'm a lefty,' I say. 'We have to switch.'

We shuffle ourselves around again. What could be worth this much effort? All the other pairs seem to be working fine and yet again I'm the awkward one who hasn't found her groove. We finally sort ourselves out. We are sitting close, but not quite shoulder to shoulder, because the extra stool sits between us.

'Do you want to draw my hand first?' He offers his hand to me, resting it on the stool between us. It sits in a loose fist, which I'm not super keen to draw. It looks tense and is adding to my sense of discomfort. Without thinking I take his hand and re-position it so the palm is facing upward, tilted to the left with fingers slightly curled.

'Better?' he asks, his eyebrow raised, and I can't quite work out whether he is annoyed or amused.

Crap. I should have asked before I moved his hand.

'Better,' I manage. I'm trying not to think about the fact that I just touched his hand.

I focus on my sketch. His nails are short but his fingers are long. His knuckles are much bigger than mine and the skin on his palm looks calloused. While I sketch his hand, I can see that although it is no longer in a fist, it's not relaxed either. Just like me, I'm not exactly relaxed. I try to draw quickly. This is what Betty was trying to achieve with her timed exercises. It's surprising. Rather than feeling worried about the marks, I'm making work without thinking. I just have to get the sketch done. After what feels like no time at all, I put down my pencil.

'Done.'

I'm still on edge. Hyperaware of everything.

I wave my right hand above the stool that sits between us. I flip it, palm side up, palm side down. Up, down, up, down. I'm not sure how he wants me to position it. It's like a fish out of water, flailing about. My hand has become the complete embodiment of how I am feeling.

'Can I?' he nods at my flipping hand.

'It's all yours.'

I try to relax my hand. He takes it, placing it palm down, then uses his whole hand to gently smooth my fingers so my hand is now completely flat. His hand is warmer than expected. His skin rougher. Sparks rise in my stomach. I look up from my hand at the same moment as he does and our eyes meet for a beat before I look away.

What was that?

I roll my shoulders up then back and down in an attempt to relax myself. My hand sits between us. I sneak a look back at Mattias. He has moved on. His eyes jump from his drawing and back to my hand. He is very easy to look at, I'll give him that. I can't help but take in the line of his jaw, the angle of his nose. But before I can work out whether he has a strong jaw or not (whatever that is, and for the record I think he does), he stops drawing and leans back ever so slightly in his chair to assess his work. Then he turns to me and I quickly look away.

'Ready,' he says. Before I can react, his hand is next to mine on the stool. His pinky brushes against mine and my stomach flips over.

It's just his pinky, for goodness' sake. Get a grip, Cleo. Just draw the boy's hand. I roll my shoulders back again. His palm rests upwards this time, in a similar position to where it was last time. An invitation to re-position.

This time I ask first. 'Do you mind?' My eyes catch his again.

He nods. Normally I'd be questioning whether a nod meant that he did mind or that he didn't, but something in his eyes tells me not to worry. I draw his pointer and middle finger in and rest his thumb over his pointer to hold them there. My fingers linger a fraction longer than necessary. His palm still faces me. It's an interesting position and will be harder to draw, but when he nods at me again, I get started.

While I sketch his hand this time, I feel his eyes on me, watching me as I'd watched him. But it's not like last time when he caught me looking at him. Something has shifted. The rest of the class fades away and all I can do is focus on his hand in this moment. We fall into a rhythm of sketching. Then slowly, gently remodelling our hand positions. Then watching each other draw. And holy crap, how has drawing someone else's hand just become the most erotic moment in my life?

I am startled when Betty claps her hands, indicating time is up. Beside me, Mattias sits up sharply. Betty's claps propel us from the moment, almost awakening us from a dream, and as Mattias turns away from me I am immediately sad to move on. To lose this moment, this connection.

It's time to pack up and I want to speak to him. More than that, I want him to speak to me. To acknowledge that I wasn't alone in the moment. That we just shared something. Even though our hands are both dropped now, it's like there is an electric current in the air. Surely it's not just me who feels it.

I have to speak. 'Mattias, um . . .' I don't know what to say.

A hand on my shoulder makes me jump.

'What's going on?' asks Lachlan. He stands between us with one hand on Mattias's shoulder too.

It's not a question that I know the answer to. And I'm not sure Mattias does either. Luckily, Lachlan is not looking for an answer to that question, he has another. 'Remi and I are headed to the Art Gallery this afternoon. Do you . . .' Lachlan pauses here. 'Uh, you two want to join us?'

I already know my answer. 'Sure, I'll be there.'

Mattias looks at his watch, then back to me. 'I've got some time this arvo.'

Chapter Twelve

The idea of a casual visit to the Art Gallery makes me feel grown up and cultured. And although I'm excited by this I also just want to pull Mattias into a quiet space and ask him what the hell that was. Or maybe I won't ask him anything, maybe I'll just wait to see what would happen if we weren't interrupted. But I can't do either of those, so for the time being, Art Gallery it is.

'It'll just take twenty-two minutes to walk up,' says Remi, consulting her phone.

'Those timeframes are always so conservative, in my experience,' Lachlan says. 'We'll get there in no time. We can beat that, can't we, Cleo?'

'Sure, I guess.'

‘Okay,’ says Lachlan. ‘I’m setting a timer.’ He fiddles with his watch. ‘You all ready? Set? Go!’ He links his arm through mine and we set off at a pace.

I look over at my shoulder at Mattias. ‘Sorry,’ I try telling him, but he walks with Remi and I can’t seem to catch his eye.

We walk for a bit and then Lachlan stops outside a convenience store. ‘What is it with you and convenience stores?’ I ask.

‘It’s all about the snacks,’ says Lachlan. ‘Every outing is better with snacks.’

It’s hard to disagree. We motion we are going inside. I want Mattias to come in as well, to walk down the narrow aisles with me, casually bumping into me, inching closer when another shopper walks past, but he stays with Remi outside.

We make good time, just beating the map’s estimate even with our additional stop.

‘I’m hungry, let’s eat now,’ says Lachlan as we stand in front of the Gallery.

‘No,’ says Remi. ‘We can sit for as long as we want after, but the Gallery will close in a bit over an hour so we don’t want to feel like we missed our chance, or that we have to leave after we just got in there.’

‘I agree, let’s go in,’ says Mattias.

'That makes sense,' I say. 'Although I am looking forward to snacks.' I give Lachlan an empathetic smile.

'Three against one,' Lachlan grumbles. 'But if you start to get hungry, just remember I was the one who said we should eat first.'

Remi leads the way through the columns at the front then through the foyer and into the Gallery. The first room opens out in front of us. It is expansive and full of work that is incredible, but also very proper and a perhaps a bit stuffy. It fits the definition of Art with a capital A. But it doesn't necessarily excite me. It doesn't leave me with questions like Louise Bourgeois' *Maman* sculpture did when we studied it at school. I wish I had seen that giant spider when it sat outside the front of the Gallery.

We wander from room to room together, separating out to look at whatever catches our eye. Sometimes I stand next to Remi and she tells me what she likes about a piece. 'Look at the light in this one, isn't it dramatic?'

'I really think this one would look great on my bedroom wall,' I say.

When my alarm goes off, it startles me for a moment, but I take my phone out quickly and silence it. I can't see a window, but thankfully I'm standing in front of a Streeton. The sky is blue in his landscape. I take a moment to stop and remember before moving on to the next piece of art.

Sometimes Mattias walks next to me, and I am alert, almost on edge, waiting for him to close the gap between us, waiting for his hand to brush against mine, like it did earlier in the day. But it doesn't and I continue on.

I catch sight of Lachlan leaning a little too close to a neoclassical painting of four nude women lounging together in a room.

'What are you doing?' I ask. 'Besides wondering what the context of this particular scene is?'

Lachlan adopts a higher voice. 'If I hold the vase like this, do you think they'll overlook the fact that I forgot my scarf?' He mimics the awkward way the woman is holding the cylindrical vase.

'Am I nailing superhero chic?' I say.

'When I'm naked with the girls I just love to roll around on . . . curtains.'

'This is an audition for *Love Island*, right?'

Lachlan chuckles. 'So, I've been playing a little game,' he says, bringing me back to the original question I asked him. 'It's inspired by class. Want to join in?'

While Lachlan is talking, I find myself scanning the room for Mattias. I can see that he's walked into the next room.

'What type of a game is it?' I ask.

'A counting one.'

'Sounds easy enough.'

'It sounds easy, but it's harder than it looks.'

I'm intrigued. 'Go on.'

'It's called Hair or Bare.'

'Okay . . .'

'How about you learn by example? So, this one's not obvious but I'm counting it as hair for two. Only just though. See? There and there? Just a skerrick. But that sculpture? He's definitely bare. Bald as. I'm currently at four hair to five bare. It's neck and neck.'

I realise what Lachlan is doing. 'Noooo,' I say. 'Ewwwww.'

Lachlan shrugs. 'It's all art. I'm just cataloguing it. Let me know if you want to play.'

After five minutes, my moral high ground gives way and I find myself checking the downstairs situation of any nude I see and comparing findings with Lachlan. At one point the security guard gives us a warning look. And when we fight over the shading on a reclining maiden and I laugh so hard I have to cross my legs so I don't pee myself, I'm afraid the security guard will kick us out.

Outside, bags of chips are torn open and I take a handful of salt and vinegar. I've chosen the good ones and they crunch so nicely. I lick the salt from my bottom lip. Next to me, Lachlan takes a handful of Cheezels, sliding his fingers through the holes.

'How old are you? Five?' I ask.

I look to Remi to back me up.

'Actually, I think at heart I'm five too, I love Cheezels.'

'No, Remi, not you too. Ugh.' I shudder. 'I can't believe you like them too. That cheese flavouring stays on your hands forever.'

'You can never pick a Cheezel lover,' Lachlan chimes in, stuffing three more into his mouth. 'How about you, Mattias, where do you stand on this important topic? Will you join the young at heart or are you stuck up and bougie in your chip choice like young Cleo over here?'

Lachlan is lying on one side, elbow propping him up. He nudges me with his foot, letting me know he's only kidding. Normally the physical contact would send me into a spin. Not today.

'I'm with Cleo,' says Mattias, finally catching my eye, and holding it for what feels like a moment too long and also not long enough. I wonder if Lachlan catches his double meaning, '*I'm* with Cleo', or if there is even a double meaning to catch.

'Put me in first class with her,' Mattias says, reaching for the salt and vinegar.

'I should have known,' says Lachlan. 'I'll bet you never got your clothes dirty when you were kids either.'

'Don't be so sure,' I say.

The afternoon sun warms my skin and I am thankful for this moment sitting with friends in a park. It's new and I love it.

'Hey, let's play a game,' says Lachlan bringing me out of my moment with the sun.

'Another one?' I ask.

'Of course, there can never be enough games. This one's called Either Or.'

Remi reaches for the Cheezels and loads up her fingers. I shudder. 'I don't know that one,' she says.

'That's because I just made it up,' says Lachlan, his face breaking into a big smile. 'We know all your answers to *either* Cheezels *or* salt and vinegar, but let's do some more. I'll go first, another easy one. Summer or winter? I'm going with summer. Remi?'

'Winter. I love ugg boots, hot beverages and curling up with a good book or my sketchpad.'

'I'm going with winter as well. My dad loved the snow and used to take me with him every year when I was little,' says Mattias. 'Cleo, what do you think?'

'I'm torn, I don't know. Can I say spring?' I answer. I have a feeling I'm going to struggle with this game.

'Cop-out,' says Lachlan. 'Boo.' I can tell he's just joking because he is smiling. 'Okay, next one, book or movie. Movie for sure for me. You guys?'

'Book,' Remi is quick to answer.

'I'm team book too,' says Mattias. Lachlan raises his eyebrows in surprise and everyone looks to me.

'Umm, I guess I like different things about both. Sometimes I just want someone to do the work for me, I just want to consume. But then there's a beauty to imagining things yourself, and honestly there are so many great books that will never leave me. But I don't think I could choose.'

Remi nods at me. 'I get it,' she says. 'Here's an easy one: fruit or vege? It's vege for me.'

'Fruit,' the boys both answer before looking at me.

'You guys, I'm terrible at this. Both are good, I can't choose. Okay, what about chocolate or ice cream?' I ask, then realise that I can't actually pick between these two either.

Remi and Mattias vote for chocolate, while Lachlan votes for ice cream.

'Pasta or rice?' asks Mattias.

Remi gestures to her face. 'Do you even have to ask? Always rice.'

'Rice for me too,' says Mattias.

'Pasta,' says Lachlan.

I laugh. 'How can you decide so easily?'

'Now what about this one,' asks Remi with one eyebrow raised, 'Liberal or Labor?'

'Urgh, I've no idea. I'm a teenager, how would I even know? I'm not political at all.' I flop down on the grass.

The grass moulds under my body and I can feel the warmth of the sun on my arms and face. 'I give up, I'm not playing anymore.'

'Labor,' says Mattias.

'Liberal,' says Lachlan.

'Labor for me,' says Remi.

'Okay, this one is harder,' says Lachlan, and I wonder how it can possibly be harder. 'God or no God?'

'God,' says Remi, sounding more certain than anyone has on anything.

I'm glad I've already passed because again I am unsure. More than unsure.

'No God,' says Lachlan.

'God, I hope,' says Mattias. 'Definitely a conversation to have later,' he says, directing his comment to Remi. 'Okay, changing the tone,' he continues, 'how about posing naked or swimming naked?'

'Swimming,' says Remi without so much as a pause.

'Remi! You? Really?' I can't believe it.

'There's something so freeing about skinny-dipping,' she says.

'Well, cold water does nothing for me, so I'm going with posing nude,' says Lachlan. 'Someone's got to think about all the art students who need models to keep their art alive. We can't have them getting stuck with this afternoon's fate of just drawing hands.'

'I happen to like drawing hands,' says Mattias, and without sitting up and looking I feel his eyes resting on me. 'Also, I'd choose skinny-dipping.'

'Neither for me,' I say, again glad to have bowed out early. The thought of stripping bare in public terrifies me, and it's not because I'm particularly body-conscious. I'm surprisingly okay with the way my body looks. I feel uncomfortable with the idea of removing everything. I don't have the confidence. I somehow have the idea that if the clothes come off, people will be able to see inside my soul too. I know it doesn't make sense. But the clothes are an extra barrier for the weakness and the grief, so they don't come busting out.

'What about . . .' says Lachlan, bringing me out of my thoughts, a wicked grin playing on his lips. 'Hair or bare?'

'Oh no,' I say, recognising where this is going.

'Huh?' says Mattias.

'Lachlan, should you be asking about pubic hair?' I say, sitting up. 'This feels way too personal.'

'I'm not quite sure how we jumped from faith to general nakedness to pubic hair,' says Remi. Her tone is even; she is neither accusing nor approving.

Mattias grimaces. 'That could be my fault, and I'm bowing out of this round. People should do what they want to do.'

I, however, do have thoughts on this. 'I'm tapping back in,' I say, causing Remi to look at me in surprise. 'The game in the Gallery was fun,' I add, and see a frown flicker across Mattias's face. 'But I think, even though we joke about it, there are some real issues here. I am hair all the way.'

'Me too,' agrees Remi, although I can see she feels a little uncomfortable, as we've perhaps given the boys a little too much information. 'What teenager has the time and money to keep on top of that?'

As she asks, I see Lachlan's hand rising as if he has an example. I shake my head. 'No, don't tell me. I don't want to know.'

'Do you think it's a porn thing?' asks Remi tentatively.

Lachlan raises his hand again, and this time I really don't want to know.

'Actually,' I say, 'my mum is a midwife, so in many ways she often gets an eyeful, and she says some women come in completely waxed before childbirth. They do that in preparation. They think it's better, cleaner maybe. But there is no reason for that, no research that says so. I think it is so unnecessary.'

'What about for swimming?' Lachlan asks finally getting a word in.

I have to admit it's actually a good point. 'Okay,' I concede, 'that is a good reason. But I just hate the idea of people, women really, thinking that's what they should do, or that's what they have to do. It just feels wrong. I mean, if that's what you want, fine. But this is one of the things that separates me from a ten-year-old. So, for me, it's all about the hair. Go Shelly!' I say referring to our model from the second day of the program. Her bush was prodigious.

I take a breath. 'The floor is yours, Lachlan: hair or bare? I hope what you're "promoting"' – I make quotation marks with my fingers – 'is what you are "sporting", if you catch my drift.'

'So, what I'm taking from this is it's okay if that's what she wants?' Lachlan answers.

'Ew, Lachlan, that's what you took from this conversation?' I ask.

Lachlan shrugs. 'You said it.'

'Amongst other things,' Remi points out. 'Which were significantly more important.'

Lachlan looks over to Mattias. 'A little backup, man?'

'Nope, you're on your own. I have no opinion. But I don't think you'll win this one,' says Mattias.

'Awwww, Lachlan, that's okay,' says Remi. 'A little humility will do you good. You can't always win.'

'Yeah, yeah,' says Lachlan, rolling his eyes and checking his phone. 'You know, I've actually got to go. I'll see you next time.' Lachlan grabs his backpack, swinging it onto his back before striding away.

The three of us still sitting exchange looks.

I hope I haven't ruined things. I start to feel that I might have. 'Did I . . .' I falter. 'Was that . . . my fault?' I haven't known Lachlan for that long but I've never seen so much as a shadow cross his face.

Mattias fixes me with his eyes. 'Cleo, he asked for your opinion, and you gave it, you can't apologise for that.'

I nod. 'I just . . .'

Remi touches her hand to my shoulder. 'No. You can't be responsible for how everyone feels about everything. He might not have agreed with you but, that's on him, not you.'

'Plus, he was the one to bring it up,' says Mattias.

'Okay. Thanks, both of you,' I say, trying to ignore the discomfort that is threatening to ruin the afternoon.

Chapter Thirteen

Despite Lachlan leaving abruptly after our conversation, I'm in a good mood as I set the table for dinner, the day's events playing through my mind. I feel excited but also somewhat confused. I'm not crazy to think that earlier in the day there was a moment, a serious moment, with Mattias, am I? And was there something at Lachlan's party? But then I wonder if I'm imagining things, because by the time we were at the Gallery it was like everything had worn off, the spark had fizzled. Although, there were times when we were out on the lawn chatting when he looked at me. And Lachlan, well, it's so easy with him, he's so much fun . . . but maybe a bit too much sometimes?

It's not a real thing, and most people would call it thinking, but in my mind, I'm monologuing this all to my sister and imagining how she would respond. It's fun to think about in this way and I know she would laugh at me and lean in and ask me for all the details about both boys. The shape of their shoulders, colour of their eyes, depth of their voice, warmth of their laugh – she would have asked for every single piece of information I knew about them and I would have been embarrassed but would have loved describing each minute detail.

Mum interrupts my imagined conversation. 'Cleo, come help me with the plates.' She calls to my dad, 'Andrew, dinner!' before thrusting two plates into my hands.

We sit and as I pour myself some water, I notice my parents exchange a look. It takes me a minute to realise why.

I've been so lost in my imagined conversation I have set the table for four people, not three. I have set the table for myself, my mum, my dad and Emmy. It's been a while since I've done this, but it used to happen all the time.

My heart sinks a little, but I try to keep it light with my parents. 'Oh well,' I say. 'I guess it's a good way to remember her, right? Maybe we should still set it for her.'

My parents exchange looks again. The worried type, like they are both acknowledging there is a problem that needs to be solved.

'Darling, I don't think we should do that,' my dad says.

'Remember what Jean said?' Mum asks.

'Your counsellor said a lot of things, Mum, and you've told me so many of them, I can't be sure which one you're referring to.'

This is both true and also not true. Mum loves to pass on *Jean*'s cliched advice, so much so that Dad and I had begun playing bingo whenever Mum uttered one of Jean's pieces of wisdom. If Mum told us that Jean had said, 'You just have to take it one day at a time,' Dad and I would shout out, 'BINGO!' We did this until I found Mum sobbing as she was sitting at her computer after one particularly loud bingo call.

'Talking to Jean helps me,' Mum had said.

From then on, Dad and I whispered our bingo calls to each other or counted them up and shared them when we next saw each other, because our bingo game was helping us.

So, when Mum asks me to remember what Jean says, it could be anything. But, if I had to put money on it, I'd bet it would be, 'Don't be afraid to move on.'

This was the one I was hearing a lot.

Mum fixes me with a soft smile. 'Darling, you can't be afraid to move on.'

'Bingo!' I mouth to Dad, but he shakes his head at me.

'She's right,' he says. 'We've got to keep going forward.'

'One day at a time?' I ask. 'One foot in front of the other?'

But he doesn't even crack a smile, much less give a bingo call.

'Yeah, but, we still have to remember. We can't just forget her.'

'None of us are forgetting her,' Dad says, his tone even. 'And it's difficult. We all acknowledge that it feels like an impossible task. And yet, we have to do it.'

'And we all agreed it's what she would have wanted,' Mum adds.

There have been many times when I wish Emmy could have written me a plan for this. 'Plan for Talking to Our Parents About My Death', or 'Plan for Doing Life Without Me'. If she had I would know exactly what she would have wanted. But she couldn't because no one knew what would happen, that she'd be here one day and gone the next.

'Darling, we are so pleased for you, this art course, it's exactly what you needed. Something different, fresh. It's been wonderful.'

Mum's maybe not completely wrong here. But I'm not about to tell her that.

We eat the rest of our dinner in silence, because it doesn't matter what they say about *moving on*. I have my own ways of *holding on*, of making sure I don't forget her.

Chapter Fourteen

Tuesday morning I am more than on time; I have time to spare. No buses are late, everything runs smoothly. I'm walking past Hyde Park, taking it slow, enjoying actually knowing where to walk. I'm a little lost in my own thoughts, a not too unusual state for me to be in, when I think I hear my name being shouted out. I can't see anyone so suspect that I'm hearing things. Then I hear it again. It's Mattias. He's standing at a coffee shop across the road waving at me.

'What are you doing?' I call out across the road. He holds up his takeaway cup by way of answer and motions for me to wait for him before heading to the crossing.

'Walk with you?' he asks, now he stands next to me.

I smack my head with my palm.

'So maybe I won't walk with you,' Mattias says.

'No, of course, sorry, let's walk,' I say, feeling stupid for overreacting. 'I left your shirt at home. I'm sorry. I forgot, I keep forgetting.' That's not quite true. It is sitting on the edge of my bed and for some reason I'm not quite ready to part with it. I don't fully understand this boy. I feel like the last time we spoke, actually had a proper conversation, just the two of us, was at the party and yet we have spent time together since then. Sometimes it's awkward talking to him and a bit frustrating but . . . for some reason I want to keep doing it. I want to know him more.

'Okay. You had me worried for a minute there.'

We turn onto Oxford Street, our footsteps falling in time.

'So, I know you like books and winter and flame trees,' I say.

'Flame trees? I do?'

'Yeah, you know, from the introductions to the class?'

'Oh yeah, I hate that sort of thing, introductions. I never know what to say.'

'Seriously? Me too, I was scrambling. You know, it's the first impression and I didn't want to say something weird. I wanted people to be like, huh, yeah, that's cool. I'd like to talk to that girl more. I wanted to make a good impression. Especially after the horror of turning up late. I mean, you sounded so resolute though. So sure of yourself.' I feel like I'm babbling but this time Mattias doesn't seem phased.

He is silent for a moment before he answers. 'It was the first thing that popped in my head. Flame trees are pretty cool, especially at this time of year. I do love a jacaranda too though.'

He remembered.

'So, what else should I know about you?' I ask. 'At Lachlan's you said that parties aren't your norm. So, what do you do when you're not hanging out in art galleries, or drawing, or un-creepily watching people dance then spilling your drinks on them?'

He knows I'm joking and his lips twitch into a grin that makes my stomach flip in a good way.

'I guess some nights I'm working, or hanging with a mate, exercising or just chilling at home. And schoolwork, obviously'

'Huh.'

'What do you mean "huh"?'

'I think that's not . . . what I expected?' My words pitch up at the end, turning my thoughts into a question.

'What did you expect?' Mattias stops walking momentarily and looks at me, waiting to see how I'll answer.

'I mean . . .' What do I mean? You know what, let's go with honesty. 'The truth?'

'Give it to me.'

I start walking again so I don't have to look at him. 'So . . . parties, the cool kids – not my vibe.' There. I said it. I admitted to not being cool. 'But you . . . I just assumed you ran with the popular crowd, you know, surrounded by all your peeps.' Why did I say that word, I'm so cringe.

Mattias laughs out loud. 'What makes you think that? You're the one who said I was a grandpa.'

A hot grandpa. I can't believe he remembers the conversation as much as I do. Is he really going to make me say it? Make me tell him he's hot? Nope. I'm not going to do it. I evade the question. 'I still stand by the grandpa bit, but maybe like a popular grandpa? With lots of friends at your school so you don't *have* to socialise with the nerdy people in your art class.' I motion at myself. Which Mattias ignores.

'You would call Imogen nerdy?'

'Not to her face.'

'You've got it totally wrong.'

'I have?'

'Absolutely.'

'So you don't sit with all the cool kids while the rest of the school wishes they could be like you?'

'Do you think high school works like that?'

'That's exactly what a cool kid would say. They are so above the system they can't see it.'

Mattias laughs again, but this time there doesn't seem to be the humour attached. He directs the conversation back to me. 'What do you do when you're not drawing nudes, dancing the night away, trying to make a decision or being a fantastic little sister?'

The question surprises me, and not only because he's remembered our conversation and summed me up fairly well but also because I don't quite know how to answer it. The answer is I'm not really sure. It's hard to work out who I am without my sister. I brush the question off. 'School, work, the usual.'

But it hasn't been. It's been two years and still nothing feels usual, nothing is normal. And if it ever does feel normal then it's important I remind myself of what I'm missing. I'm not keen to go there, not keen to talk about it. I don't want to think about who I am without my sister. I need to change the subject again. I say the first thing that pops into my head.

'So do you have a super cool girlfriend who sits at your lunch table with you and all your super popular friends?' I regret the question immediately. Why the heck did I say that? Why did I have to ruin our perfectly normal conversation? Maybe it's the fact that somehow as we walk our shoulders are bumping against each other and I don't want to imagine someone else standing so close to him.

'No.'

No she doesn't sit with you or no she doesn't exist? The question sits on the edge of my tongue but this time I don't let it slip. I hold it in with my breath as I wait for his answer. Why am I so invested?

'I don't have a girlfriend,' he says, and I let the breath out. 'I mean, obviously I'm amazing at talking to girls. I make them feel at ease right away. I never hang back and let them talk to others when I want to talk to them. I never say dumb shit, spill drinks or talk about liking trees,' he says with a wry laugh.

'Obviously. No, who would do that?' I answer with a chuckle. 'Also, nothing wrong with liking trees,' I add.

'Do you ever draw trees?' he asks. 'That's what I was thinking about when I said flame trees. I can see one from my bedroom window and it's the one thing that I come back to time and time again to draw. It's almost like I can track my own growth and change as I draw its changes.'

It's the openness and vulnerability that surprises me most. I answer without thinking.

'We had a jacaranda tree out the front of my place. I haven't drawn it, but every year when the tree is in full bloom my sister and I would take photos together. I guess it also serves as a marker in our family. At least it did.'

Mattias doesn't press the issue. We walk the rest of the way in silence, careful not to step in the way of the busy foot traffic. It reminds me of the closeness of our first morning at the Art School, our shoulders touching, heat building in my leg, and of our time drawing together.

When we get to the door, Mattias pauses before going in. 'Hey, if you want to come draw trees with me some time,' he says, 'let me know?'

I bite my bottom lip, stopping the smile that threatens to blanket my entire face.

'Sure. I could do that.'

'Should I take your number?'

'Yeah, good idea,' I say deliberately, not mentioning that I could probably find him on the group chat Lachlan set up. I fumble my phone out of my back pocket. 'I'll grab yours too.' I unlock my phone and open a new contact before passing it to him. He takes it in his left hand and passes me his phone. As I type my name and contact number, I feel a flicker of excitement.

Lachlan is there waiting for us when we get in. 'Hey,' he says, and sets himself up next to me once I've chosen my spot.

I'm still not super happy with how he reacted to the conversation we had yesterday, or the fact that he even asked that question at all, but his smile is so charming I find it hard to do anything else but smile back.

When Remi walks in, Lachlan says, 'Cleo, I wanted to wait till Remi got here, but I hope there's no hard feelings after yesterday. I don't want you to think badly of me. I get a bit carried away sometimes.'

I'm relieved to hear him say this. It feels like the air has been cleared.

Remi seems to agree and nods her appreciation to Lachlan, then we get ready for the day ahead.

The message comes when I'm on the train headed home. When I see his name, I laugh. *Mattias (Not a Grandpa).* I didn't see the name he'd put into my contacts list. I feel a flutter of excitement.

Hey, if you need a break from drawing nudes and want to draw something different, I'm thinking of taking a walk with my sketchbook on Saturday. Want to join?

The speed at which my heart is now beating confirms that, yes, I definitely do want to join. But should I text back now or play it cool? Don't overthink it, I tell myself.

Sure, that'd be fun. I hit send.

Come to my place and head out from there? Say 12:30?

He texts me his address and I immediately, madly, google how to get there.

Chapter Fifteen

Mum's eyes widen when I ask if I can use the car to drive to Helensburgh. I've not had my licence for long and the very thought of driving somewhere outside my comfort zone is enough for the onset of cold sweats. Mum knows how I feel driving to new places. She knows that I am more worried about finding myself in the wrong lane and heading in the wrong direction in a car than I am about almost anything else. So, she is remarkably restrained when she says, 'Sure, darling, do you want me to help you work out how to get there?'

In the past, Emmy would have helped me out, either come with me or dropped me off, but obviously that's not possible now. I don't feel like I can ask my mum to drive me. She dropped me in Caringbah last weekend and I don't want to appear like I'm six years old. This time public transport is just not viable. It'd take almost three times as long via public transport. Driving is the only option.

I study the way before I leave. I've almost memorised the turns and have written them out on Post-its. I wish I could just use apps on my phone, but I have heard too many stories about P-platers getting busted for using their phones and I'm possibly even more freaked out about being pulled over by the police than I am about going the wrong way, which is saying something. Before I leave, Mum pulls me into a hug. 'I'm proud of you,' she says into my hair. 'And if you feel worried, find a safe place to pull over. Turn the car off and check your phone. Also please let me know when you get there.'

I wish I had some sassy comeback but it's taking almost all my effort to keep calm enough to get into the car. 'Thanks, Mum,' is all I can manage.

I check the map one more time before pulling out of the drive, but by the time I turn onto the highway I still have to work hard to convince myself that the nervous poo I need to do is all in my head. Fifteen minutes into the drive my pits are wet, despite the fact that the aircon is blasting and I haven't taken a wrong turn.

Forty minutes later I've taken two wrong turns and have had to pull over to check my location.

Fifty-seven minutes later I've arrived. I take a moment before getting out of the car to congratulate myself for making it and to get a grip on my situation. I'm at a boy's house. Ready to spend the day with him. Not just any boy, either. One who I really like and who maybe, just maybe, might be interested in me. I quickly get my phone out and message my mum to tell her I've made it.

I am only just out of the car when Mattias opens the door to his house. The smile on his face is infectious. He heads down to the kerb to meet me and I go into momentary panic mode. How do I greet him? What even am I to him? It's moments like these where I long for super clear-cut greeting rules. I've been told that in some countries people bow to greet each other, some they kiss each other on the cheek once, others three times. Mattias's arm is extended and I don't know if we are shaking hands or hugging. I'm probably overthinking it. I go in for the hug then freak out and give him the world's weirdest high five.

He looks at me and laughs, but not in a mean way. 'What was that?'

'I don't know,' I admit. 'I panicked. I'm still in my slightly angsty driving headspace.' I look up at him, and his eyes are shining. 'Want a redo?' I ask.

'Sure.'

'Okay, but you have to make it clear how you're going to greet me, or I'll mess it up again.'

'What if we have a special handshake? You know, like those teachers you see on socials who memorise a unique greeting for each of their students.'

This time it's my turn to laugh. 'I could get around that,' I say. 'But no shaking feet, that's just strange.'

We end up deciding on a high five that continues into a low five, a weird elbow pump, then linking arms and spinning each other round in a circle. 'This is even odder than shaking each other's feet,' I say.

'Agreed, but probably more fun,' he says, his arm still linked through mine. 'Want to come in for a drink or something before we head out?' He escorts me up the path to his front door and opens it for me. 'I'm glad you made it, Cleo.'

'Were you worried I wouldn't come? That I'd stand you up?'

I immediately regret using those words. I've just turned our casual hang into a date.

Mattias appears to properly consider the question but doesn't query my word choice. 'I don't think so; should I have been?'

I consider telling him about my track record when driving to new places. It's not something I'm proud of. 'No, I was looking forward to it.'

Mattias's house is small, but with big windows and lots of light. I drink a glass of water standing at the kitchen bench. I feel the intimacy of being invited inside his house, of getting to see another layer of him. 'Did you grow up in this house?' I ask.

'I did,' he answers. 'Only house I've ever lived in.'

When I ask for directions to the bathroom, he points me down the hall and I stall there for a moment before heading back out.

'I thought we could head down south a bit and walk along the coast. Then if we see something we want to draw we can just stop,' Mattias says, checking in with me. His car keys jingle in his hand and he has a backpack hanging over one shoulder.

'Sounds great.'

In the car, I watch Mattias place his arm over the back of my seat then turn to look behind him as he reverses his car out into the street. It's nice to see him in his natural environment. For some reason he seems more at ease. More himself maybe.

'Do you like driving?' I ask.

'I do, I like the independence of it. Just being able to pick up and go. It might sound stupid, but it makes me feel grown-up.'

'Nah, that's not stupid, I actually just like holding car keys in my hands, that in itself makes me feel grown-up.

It's not something I feel very often, so I have to hold onto it when it comes,' I say.

Mattias chuckles. 'Why don't you feel grown-up?'

'Are you sure you want to know the answer to this? You might get an insight into my messy brain that you wish you didn't get.'

'Hit me with it, I might like your messy brain.'

His eyes are on the windy road and I want to ask him *What does that even mean?* right away, but I file it away to revisit later. Instead, I say, 'I think I spend most of my life either paralysed with indecision or feeling like kicking myself for making the wrong decision and I'm terrible at being by myself.' I pause for a beat. 'Sometimes I think I'm even terrible at being myself.'

'Did you ever think that might be how adults feel all the time too? I'm not sure if that's strictly a kid or teenage problem.'

'Huh.' No, I hadn't considered that at all. I make another mental note to ask my mum about it.

I put my window down when we hit the Sea Cliff Bridge. The completely apt name does not do justice to the beauty of this stretch of road that transports us over the intersection between the sea and the cliff edge of the Escarpment. I rest my elbow on the car's window frame, cup my chin in my hand and take it in.

'Beautiful corner of the world,' says Mattias.

'Sure is,' I reply. I feel the breeze on my face and take in the moment, and we fall into silence for the rest of the drive.

We pull off the road and Mattias parks the car in a small car park near a playground and a preschool.

'Wow!' I say. 'Imagine going to preschool there. What a view.'

'It's pretty great.' Mattias catches my eye and for a second I'm not sure if he's referring to the view or me, and I feel flustered.

'Shall we walk?' I ask as I gather my gear together.

'Yep, let's do it. Let me know if you want to stop for something.'

The footpath takes us up and down and winds around next to the road. As it narrows, Mattias walks ahead of me when a girl on an e-bike comes hurtling by and again when couple of runners shoot past us, panting as they go.

We walk past a surf lifesaving club and I ask, 'Do you surf, Mattias?'

'Not anymore,' says Mattias.

'Why's that?'

'Well, I guess to cut a long story short it was something I did with my dad when he still lived with us, but after he left, continuing on just didn't feel right.

Sometimes another friend's dad would take us out, but I'd spend the whole session wishing it was *my* dad with us and forget to just enjoy being out there. It got to the point where even the thought of it made me sad, you know? So I stopped.'

'That makes sense,' I say. But then I ask, 'Do you think that's always the right answer? If something feels sad just to stop? I just wonder, if it was an activity you liked then, why should you miss out?'

Mattias thinks for a moment. 'No, it's definitely not always the right answer. But I think in this case it was. I liked going surfing with my dad but I think it was the dad bit rather than the surfing bit that I particularly enjoyed. I liked going with *him*. But then I just started to resent surfing, if you really want to know. I felt like Dad put it before me; I started to feel like he liked it more than me.'

'That's pretty rotten,' I say. 'I'm sorry you felt like that. What a sucky way to feel about your dad.' I try to lighten the mood. 'I always kind of wanted to learn,' I say. 'But if I do I promise not to like surfing more than you.'

Mattias is still walking ahead of me and I wonder if what I said was perhaps a little much. He turns around and says, 'I'll hold you to that.' He smiles at me and my heart speeds up.

'What sport do you do then, if you don't surf?' I ask.

'Well, a few different things, especially as a kid, but I ended up doing a fair bit of parkour and now I'm doing more callisthenics kind of workouts.'

'Parkour, like where you run up walls and flip over?' I ask.

'Kinda,' he says with a chuckle.

We come to a stop at a beach that stretches out before us.

'Where are we now?' I ask.

'This is Sharkies,' says Mattias.

'Sorry, Sharkies?' I say. 'The beach is called Sharkies? Why are there people in the water at a beach called Sharkies? How does that make any sense?'

Mattias just laughs, and directs me towards the grassy expanse at the northern end of the beach, where we sit. 'Are you hungry, Cleo?' he asks, opening his backpack and beginning to pull food out. 'Sorry, it got a bit past lunchtime.'

'You've packed a picnic?' I ask.

'I guess. I thought we might need something. But I'm not sure you could classify this as a picnic. You have the choice between a peanut butter or Vegemite,' he says, tipping the sandwiches out of his bag. 'I've also got some apples and . . .' He pulls a bag of chips out with a flourish. 'Salt and vinegar chips.'

Warmth spreads through my body. 'That's a pretty decent picnic.' I take the peanut butter sandwich and look directly at him. 'Thank you, Mattias, that's really thoughtful,' I say, my words sounding slightly more formal than I intend.

He holds my gaze for a moment before looking back to the food and selecting the remaining sandwich. 'You're welcome, Cleo.'

We sit, backs to the sun, our feet dangling in the water of the ocean pool, having walked back to Wombarra. The contrast between the cold water and the hot sun is delicious.

'We got a good day,' says Mattias. 'This pool sits a bit closer to the sand so doesn't get the same effect of the tide that the others do.'

'How do you mean?' I ask.

'Without the tide to flush the water out every so often this one is more likely to get that little bit murkier, smellier, collect more seaweed. I think there must have been a king tide recently. It's washed the pool out.'

'King tide, I salute you,' I say, raising my hand up to my temple in a mock gesture. I rest my hands behind me, leaning back slightly on my arms. Mattias is already sitting like this and my pinky brushes against his. I don't look at him but am feeling bold, so rather than pulling away I leave it there, resting next to his. Connecting us. After a moment, his pinky moves slightly, wrapping over mine, locking us together. Sunglasses on, I turn my face to the sky. I'm not sure I've ever existed more fully in a moment than the one I am in now.

I glide my legs back and forth through the water, lifting them marginally higher than the water line before dropping them back down. Mattias does the same. His rhythm matches mine, legs moving in time. I simultaneously feel like a child, joy building inside me, and completely grown-up, a want for more also building.

I note the similarities between our legs, and the differences. His legs are more olive. Mine smoother. His more muscular.

I can hear the gulls on the shore. We have stopped swinging our legs, but somehow my left ankle is now curled around Mattias's right ankle. In the water, his foot gently presses down on mine. I swallow.

'Cleo,' says Mattias.

I turn to look at him. He holds my gaze, then his eyes drop to my lips and back up to my eyes. My heart is beating so hard I imagine it's pumping twice as much blood around my body as usual. I can't believe I didn't notice it before, but he has faint freckles on his cheeks. I bite my bottom lip, drawing his gaze back towards my mouth. I don't ever want to exist in a moment outside of this one. Except, except, to see what lies on the other side.

I lean in ever so slightly, an invitation for him to close the gap between us. My breath catches.

I feel his breath, soft on my face. He raises his right hand, traces his thumb down my jawbone. Pausing, so it rests right on the edge of my lips –

And my phone trills.

The sound startles us both.

Mattias draws back.

I look over my shoulder to where my bag sits, confirming that the tone is in fact coming from my bag. It is. Damn it.

'Did you want to get that?' Mattias asks.

No. I really don't. 'I'll leave it,' I say.

But it doesn't stop.

'I think maybe, you might need . . .' Mattias trails off, and I hear the reluctance in his voice. He releases my foot from his. Unhooks his pinky.

'I'm sorry,' I say. I stand up and go to my bag. 'Let me take a look.'

My phone continues while I unzip the pocket and fumble it out of the bag.

It's not till I look at the screen that it dawns on me.

Chapter Sixteen

My alarm.

It's my alarm and I had forgotten. How could I have forgotten?

I feel . . . sick. It's like I have just swallowed a stone and yet weirdly have way too much saliva in my mouth. I can't believe I forgot.

'Cleo, are you okay?' asks Mattias as I put my phone away. 'You look a little pale, is something wrong?'

'No,' I say. But that doesn't quite ring true because I am horrified at myself. How could I have forgotten? I can't breathe. 'Um, I just need a minute, hang on . . .'

I look up to the sky and think. But in my mind, all I can see is Mattias, his hand entwined with mine, his foot against mine in the water, and how come I can't recall a single memory? All I can think about is this boy and it should feel light, like bubbles of champagne popping inside me, but instead my heart now feels heavy. My body feels heavy. Guilt, a weighted blanket over my shoulders. Pushing me down, making me sweat. Because when I am thinking of him, I can't think of her. A bead of sweat trickles down my neck. I sink to the ground. I have failed her.

'Cleo, who is calling you? No one should make you feel like this.' Mattias's voice is soft.

'It's no one.'

'It's obviously not no one.'

I can't look at him. I don't want to see the concern on his face. And I can't convince him that it is actually no one, there is no one calling me.

'Do you need to call them back? I'll give you some space.'

If only I could just call her back.

'Can I do anything?' asks Mattias.

I don't answer straight away. I'm trying to think of her, trying to find a memory. Her tenth birthday party? What did she do for that? I can't remember. Her ordering her collection of Beanie Boos, organised by date of birth? No, that was me, not her. Why can't I think of anything? Why does it feel like I've lost her all over again?

I don't know how to tell him. I press my fingers into my temple, tying to kickstart a memory. I can't see her, but I can see that Mattias is waiting for an answer.

'I'm just. It's just . . .' How do I explain it? How do I tell him what I do? I've never told anyone. Not even my mum and dad.

Mattias looks worried. 'Shall I take you back?'

This is a question I can answer. I nod my head.

We walk quickly back from the beach, up the hill, past the playground and to the car. Then we drive in silence.

I feel a sense of relief when I see my car. Its familiarity triggers my memories. I remember how Emmy learnt to drive, my dad in the front seat, me in the back when they let me. I remember the time when she drifted a little too close to the car next to her when driving round a roundabout, and the other driver's alarm, clearly displayed on his face, and Dad making her pull over as soon as he could. 'Want a break?' he'd asked.

'Seems like it's not a break I need but more practice,' she had answered, which I found brave.

Everything inside me stiffens again. Maybe those memories are not the best ones.

I get out of his car, unlock mine and throw my stuff in.

Things are awkward with Mattias and I can't fix them. But I have managed to hold onto my sister again and that's what I need to do.

I climb into the front seat. I have to check the directions but I'm pretty sure I know where I'm going. I put my seatbelt on and start the car so I can wind down the window. 'It's right, left, left, isn't it?' I ask. Mattias is standing next to my car door. 'To get to the main road?'

'You got it,' he says.

I'm about to start the engine when I realise I haven't even said goodbye.

'I'm sorry,' I say. And I am. 'I'm sorry this didn't work. See you in class?'

'Yep,' he says.

'Bye, Mattias.'

He half smiles. 'Next time. You'd better go, Cleo.'

He seems disappointed.

I pull out and take the first right. Then, one street away I pull over. I park outside some random house. I rest my head against the side window and look up. I think about every memory I have of Emmy and me in the back seat of the car. There are a lot. Remembering her makes me feel better, much better. The guilt lifts and I am okay again.

Two years ago, when Emmy died, the house felt impossibly quiet, its stillness unnerving. The bustle was gone. There was no chatter and when someone spoke, they seemed to emphasise the emptiness, their voice bouncing off the walls.

When she was gone, the mornings were the hardest. We used to fight over the bathroom, pushing each other out of the way so we could fix our hair or wash our faces. I remember brushing my teeth one morning, spitting out my toothpaste and looking up expecting to see Emmy reflected next to me in the mirror, hands covered in product, scrunching her curls. Instead, I was alone. I would never see her fixing her hair again. I would never bump her out of the way again.

That morning, instead of putting my uniform on I went back to bed. But I didn't go to sleep, just lay there, wet spots forming on my pillow.

Neither Mum nor Dad made me go to school and by lunchtime I was still lying there. From my bed I watched the clouds forming different shapes and moving across the sky. Marshmallows became elephants doing handstands then turned into dancing teacups, which triggered a thought. Didn't Emmy like to look at the sky too? What was it that she did?

I dug in my cupboard for the shoebox of plans we had made over the years until I found it, in the very first plan, *Plan for Starting Somewhere New.* Emmy said she used to stop once a day to look at the sky. It hit me that I could do it too. This was the way I could remember my sister, hold on to her. But I had to do it every day, because memories can be tricky things.

I knew that memories fade, the colour seeps out, the impact leeches away, they become hazy and we start to question them. I knew that the further from the memory we are, the harder it is to maintain, so I knew I had to be disciplined.

I wrote my first ever plan. A simple one. I typed it up to make it official.

Plan For Making Sure Emmy Stays with Me

By Cleo Markson for herself, in order to remember Emmaline Markson

1. *Set phone alarm for 4.00 pm daily.*
2. *When the alarm goes off, stop what you are doing.*
3. *Look up at the sky if you can. (This is what Emmy did, it will help you to feel connected to her and also keep you from getting distracted.)*
4. *Choose a memory you have of your sister and play it in your mind. It's a little like studying for a test: the more you replay something, think through the details, the more you will remember. If you do this, she will stay with you forever.*

Just the act of writing the plan made me feel connected to her, so I felt that it would work. And it did. Every day I would come home from school and before going to work or to the pool my alarm would go off and I'd look at the sky and think about my sister.

Mum and Dad have told me that before digital TV, and before DVDs, there were VHS tapes. When these videos were played too many times they began to weaken, to stop working. But the tape in my mind works differently. Each play strengthens the memory, adds detail. Each play makes sure I don't forget her, that she stays with me. And it is the singular most important part of my day.

But today, when my alarm sounded, I didn't recognise it. I couldn't place it. I didn't realise it was mine. I was so caught up in the moment that my mind tripped. And when it found its footing again, I panicked because I was forgetting her. I was moving on and forgetting her and I knew I couldn't let that happen. I had vowed not to move on, no matter how often I was told to.

As I drive further away from Mattias, my resolve hardens. I can't forget my sister again.

Chapter Seventeen

My mum is in the kitchen when I get home. She looks up when I come in, confusion clear on her face.

'You're home earlier than expected. How did everything go?'

I don't answer straight away. I'm not sure what to say.

Mum stops unpacking the dishwasher and dries her hands. I still don't speak. She looks at me, really looks at me. 'Are you okay?' she asks.

If I am ever feeling the slightest bit off and someone asks me if I'm okay, it totally wrecks me. Any resolve I have to soldier on is broken down with these three words.

Normally I'd be in tears. I screw my face up, not to cry but to think about the answer. I go as close to the truth as I can.

'It was weird. I mean it started well, but I think I've realised it's not for me.'

'Did he hurt you? Do something to you? If he did, it's important to tell someone. You can't suffer in silence.'

'No, Mum! Nothing like that.' I repeat what I told her before. 'It's just not for me.'

'Okay,' says Mum, and I can see she's trying to understand what I've said. 'Do you mean he's not for you? Or . . . dating? Or . . .' She pauses again here. 'Or boys in general?'

'Mum! This is not one of those conversations,' I say. 'Look, I'm fine. You know I normally start crying if I'm not. It's just not going to work. I can't do that sort of relationship now. I don't have' – I wave my hand around the top of my head – 'like, capacity, brain space? I don't need it. It's decided.'

I can't quite read my mum's expression. 'Fine,' she says. 'If that's what you think is best.' I'm not sure she thinks it's best, but I don't care. I know what moving on cost me today.

'Look, Mum, I can still have fun, and I'm doing the art thing, I'm halfway through and it's been good, like you said, you were right. But . . . you know I've got other things that I have to focus on.'

My mum likes being right. I can see her visibly perk up, worry sliding off her. 'Okay, darling.' Then she crosses the room, comes around to the other side of the bench and gives me a hug. Still holding onto my arms, she squeezes me gently. 'You let me know if you need to talk at all though, won't you? About any of those things?'

Mum looks like she wants to say something else as well, but she bites her lip instead, physically stopping herself.

My phone chimes.

It's Mattias.

Thanks for a fun day. Hope everything is alright. Sorry you had to duck out but hope you got back home okay.

He's making it much lighter than it was. Minimising the moment, saving me from any embarrassment I might feel. It's really sweet and my heart squeezes. No boy has looked out for me like this before.

'Are you going to message him back?' asks my Mum, unselfconsciously reading over my shoulder.

'Mum! A little privacy please,' I say with more intensity than I actually feel. My mum leans back, raising her hands in surrender. I should feel pleased that he has messaged; I do feel pleased. And yet, I can't let things go any further.

Chapter Eighteen

Both Remi and Mattias are already in class when I arrive on Monday morning. They are chatting. The sight of Mattias gives me butterflies, but I remind myself that there can't be anything there.

He gives me a wave and I reply with a weak smile. It's not great. Can Remi sense the weird vibes between us?

Mattias pulls his water bottle out of his backpack. 'I'm going to fill my bottle up. Does anyone else need any water?' he asks.

'I'm good,' I say.

Remi rustles in her bag. 'Oh thanks,' she says. 'Mine was lower than I thought.' She passes her bottle to Mattias.

Once he's out of earshot, she says, 'What was up with that?'

My face gives away my mixed feelings.

Remi sucks air in through her teeth. 'That bad, huh?'

'Maybe.'

'Okay, I have an idea,' says Remi.

'Yes . . .' I say, caution evident in my voice.

'It's a fun one,' says Remi. 'I think it is, anyway. I was planning on taking a trip to Bondi, going to the markets and hanging at the beach. It's supposed to be hot this weekend. Did you want to come with?'

'Actually, that sounds really fun.' The fact that Remi wants to spend time with me warms my insides. But after my trip to see Mattias, I can't help but be cautious. Is this another new thing? Another distraction? 'What sort of timing are we thinking?'

'Well, the markets open at 10.00, and I think it's best to be there early in the day. So . . . I think if we try to get to the Junction by 9.00 or 9.30? Yeah, that'd probably work well. And I need to be back home around 5.00, I think, but that'd be enough time to make a day of it. Obviously, we can go home whenever. What do you think?'

'That'd be really fun, I'd love to go,' I say really meaning it. Plus, Mum would be happy with another outing with friends, and, if need be, I can leave before 4.00 so there isn't a repeat of alarmgate.

'Where would you love to go, Cleo?' Lachlan has arrived and made his presence known.

'Cleo and I are going to hit up Bondi Beach and the markets on Saturday,' Remi explains.

'That sounds great,' Lachlan says. 'Can I come too?'

I turn to Lachlan. 'You're like a puppy, you know that?'

'Because everyone wants to pat me?' he says.

'Because you're relentless and always underfoot?' suggests Remi.

'No, just always eager and ready to bring the fun,' I say.

'Awww, thanks, Cleo,' says Lachlan, wrapping his arms around me, picking me up and spinning me round and round. I laugh.

'See, this is exactly what I mean,' I say.

That's when Mattias walks back in.

He locks eyes with me momentarily and then looks away. I feel like I've somehow betrayed him. Lachlan is still holding me in a bear hug, my legs dangling. I whack Lachlan on the shoulder to put me down.

Mattias passes Remi's bottle back to her.

'Where do you think you'll set up?' I ask.

There is a spot next to Lachlan that is empty but Mattias gestures over to the other side of the room where there are a bunch of free easels. 'I think I'll go for a different angle today,' he says.

I watch him set up, hoping he'll look at me and smile and then I can then go and apologise for not answering his text. I think I'm ready to do that at least.

'You should ask him to come too,' Remi says quietly to me nodding in Mattias's direction.

'Oh, yeah,' I say, trying to play it cool. 'That'd be good.'

'Maybe you should go ask him now?' suggests Remi. But before I get the chance, Betty comes in and calls us to order.

Betty claps her hands to draw our session to a close. 'Now before we finish for the morning, I wanted to give you two important pieces of news or maybe information. They are connected and the reason for the first is actually the second.' There are slight frowns of confusion around the room.

'Okay, that was a touch more obtuse than it needed to be. The first is that we have a bit of an excursion, or field trip if you will, tomorrow. We are going to the Museum of Contemporary Art. We will have our usual class up until after the lunch break, then will head across to Circular Quay via public transport. There is the additional option of having dinner together, so let me know ahead of time if you think you will make the dinner and I will book a table.' People smile and nod. The noise level in the room rises and Betty waits until we settle to share the second item of news.

'The reason for going to the gallery is twofold. Firstly, we will take a look at an exhibition a friend of mine has put together, and secondly, my hope is this might prepare you a little for the exhibition that we will have here.' The noise rises again. Betty raises her hand to silence us.

'From the work that you have done, you'll each be choosing four pieces to show. Your work should have a point of connection. I'd like you to consider not just your four best pieces, but which pieces fit together as a collection. Perhaps they are all of the same model. Perhaps they all use the same medium. Perhaps you want to focus on a specific part of the body. Perhaps you will choose only pieces that convey a certain mood. It is up to you. You will all have an allocated section of wall and you can decide how to hang your work. Additionally, you will come up with a title that expresses what you think your work is saying. We will work on our exhibition pieces in the second half of each of our remaining days together. I have handouts that reiterate all this information. You can each take one.' Betty pauses to get a pile of pages from her bag. She hands it to Imogen, who is to her left. 'Take a moment to read through this and begin ideating before heading out to lunch.'

Remi turns to me. 'What an excellent opportunity. I think this'll be great chance to look at what we've already made in a new way.'

'You sound like Betty,' chimes in Lachlan.

'You know, Lachlan, I'm not embarrassed to be excited about this,' says Remi, eyeballing Lachlan fiercely, as if daring him to say more.

'Sorry, sorry,' says Lachlan. 'It'll be good. I'll grab us the sheets.'

'My family are out this week,' says Remi as we look at the information. 'It's one of the reasons why I'm keen to do something this Saturday. Do you want to stay over tomorrow night, then come to class with me on the Wednesday?' she asks, looking at me. 'It'll cut down on your travel time that evening and the next morning. And we can hang out. If you want?'

'That would be amazing,' I say, pleased to realise that I actually mean it and feel excited about these plans.

Chapter Nineteen

On Tuesday afternoon, Remi, Lachlan and I walk to Taylor Square to wait for the 333 bus. Betty has given us an hour to take a break and to get ourselves down to the Museum of Contemporary Art. I'm a little disappointed that Mattias isn't walking with us. This trip to an art gallery feels different to the last, updated but in the worst way.

I know I should have spoken to Mattias today, and I wanted to, but I just couldn't work out what to say to him.

'Did you look up the exhibition Betty wants us to see?' asks Remi, drawing me back to the surface.

'No,' I say. 'Should I have?'

'No, no,' Remi reassures me. 'I'll be interested to know if anyone has. In fact, sometimes it's nice to go in with no expectations at all. You know, experience it as it comes.'

'I think that's just about my life motto,' Lachlan says.

It surprises me to think that I haven't felt the need to look it up. That I haven't needed to prepare myself for what is coming. It feels unlike me and yet somehow freeing, considering I tend to research and then imagine most new experiences before I face them. That said, I have had other things on my mind.

While we walk, I swing my bag around and take out my phone so I can silence the alarm when it sounds.

'You two go ahead, I just have to check something,' I say to the others. I walk slightly behind them and take a moment to recall a memory with Emmy before the alarm even goes off. Is there one from the city? What about when our parents took us to the Darling Harbour water park? We were eight and ten and felt far too old for it. But Mum and Dad had made the effort to do something with us, so Emmy took me by the hand and then somehow managed to run leaf boat competitions with a bunch of the other kids who were playing there. The memory makes me smile.

When I walk into the exhibition, I know why Remi asked the question. Judging by our class's reaction, Remi is one of only two students who had thought to look up what

Betty has brought us to. The exhibition is housed in one gallery room, illuminated by red lighting. The effect is unsettling. On a plaque outside the room we see the title of the body of work and the artist's name. *There's Always Womb? Natasha Shandinni.* Underneath it reads, 'To be female is to give. Through our lives we pour ourselves out for others, living with the motto that there's always room. We give till we have nothing left. Till we are laid bare. Empty from inside out. These works serve as a reminder that we need to remember to receive. Because there won't always be womb.'

We enter this exhibition almost solemnly, feeling as if we are stepping into something important.

As we walk around the room we are treated to giant female nudes, and I can see why Betty would want us to see them for ourselves. The images are somehow beautiful yet also confronting. The women are pictured in everyday situations, their lack of dress contrasting with the world around them, the title of each artwork highlighting and, in some cases, clarifying what the woman is giving. One is titled *Everything* and shows a pregnant nude on a bus full of dressed passengers. Another is titled *Friendship*, another *Charity*, another, titled *Pleasure*, feels almost pornographic. The artwork where the woman and presumably mother plays with a toddler is called *Superannuation*, which I don't fully understand.

Whereas the nudes we have been drawing present the beauty of the body, these feel uncomfortable. It doesn't feel right to have these women naked alongside others who are fully clothed. It feels unequal, as if each woman no longer has any power within the situation. Added to this, each work has a drip or a spill somewhere on the page. Red paint running from the top left corner. Drips dropped across the middle of another.

Betty questions us as we walk round studying the images. 'While you look, I want you to think, "Why has the artist used nudes in these works?" What is the artist challenging here? Why do you think she chose the title *There's Always Womb?*? Is this a statement or a question?'

Another voice joins Betty's to ask, 'What's with the red paint?'

'A good question,' says Betty. 'I want you to think about the title of the exhibition. Its reference to a female organ is vital here in understanding the use of the red fluid.'

'Did she just say fluid?' I hear someone whisper.

'Oh,' exclaims someone else.

'That's disgusting,' says another voice.

It reminds me of a picture book called *The Giving Tree* by some American author. I remember my English teacher presenting it to our class in year 7 as an example of how an author can tell a simple story while simultaneously presenting the audience with a message or commentary. It still sticks in my mind because of the ridiculous author photo on the back of the book. I think the artist, Natasha Shandinni, is leaning into the themes of the book. A big F You to all of society who see women as beings from whom they can take, expecting them to give until they can't anymore.

We spend twenty minutes in that room alone. Looking at the artist's technique. Thinking about the questions Betty has asked. Most of the time we remain quiet. This is an exhibit with purpose, and it almost feels like cracking jokes or discussing it in there would be disrespectful to the artist.

Bursting out of the gallery into the sunshine of the early evening feels strange. Like our experience inside has disconnected us from the outside world. It feels wrong for the sun still to be up and for there to be the hustle and bustle around the harbour. Like the world should have gone quiet while we were in the gallery and yet hasn't. I link arms with Remi and we walk side by side towards the restaurant Betty has booked for us.

There are ten of us all up who have decided to stay for dinner and we are seated as one big group around two tables pushed together. The restaurant is busy.

We are handed broadsheet-sized menus designed to look like newspapers. I settle on the Thai spiced chicken burger then regret it immediately when Remi orders the apple and cinnamon pancakes.

When all the ordering is done, Lachlan fixes Betty with a stare. 'Betty, you could have at least warned us.'

Betty raises her eyebrows. 'I'm not sure I know what you mean.'

'Come on, Betty, that was not what we were expecting – right?' says Lachlan, looking around for backup.

There are a few nods around the table.

'Was it not an exhibition of nudes?' asks Betty. 'What did you think it would be?'

This stalls Lachlan for a moment. 'Well, yes, but . . . I think I was expecting a more polished version of what we were doing.'

There are more nods.

'The reason I brought you here is to show you something that your art education at school should have already taught you. Art is at its best when it makes you feel something. It could be as simple as awe at the technical skill of the artist, surprise at the interesting concept, or a sense of peace or bliss the artwork brings, but it can be much more than that too. Exceptional art can make you feel outraged, or make you feel like you finally understand something. It can present you with a new idea or a thought you hadn't considered before, or it can answer a question you've always had. Sometimes all it does is make you ask questions. It can provide you with a sense of satisfaction or unbalance you. What effect did today's exhibit have on you all?'

'It put me off balance,' says Amina. 'I think that was the red lighting.'

I speak up. 'But that was the point. It was about that lack of balance. One side taking and one side giving, things not ever being equal. The effect of the lighting is meant to mirror the purpose of the exhibition.'

'But is life always like that?' asks Imogen.

'I think sometimes it is,' I say. 'But hopefully not always. And where's the power in an artwork that says, "It *sometimes* feels like I am looking after *some* of the people around me and *maybe* it'd be good if more than two people thought about me?"'

This gets a laugh from Betty. 'Great point, Cleo. Art should make you feel but often will have something to say as well.'

I catch Mattias looking at me. I look away as soon as our eyes meet.

The conversation continues around me, questions and laughter passing around the table.

'So, was it paint or blood?' Kiaan asks.

'What do you think?' answers Betty, which causes us to fall silent.

'I think that you're probably not going to tell us,' says Lachlan, just as the waiter appears with some of the dishes we have ordered.

As we come out of the restaurant, Remi and I pause for a moment and look out over the harbour. The light has disappeared and the water is dark, we hear it lapping against the harbour's edge. I love this city so much in the daytime; I love the expanse of the sky hurled out over the water. Nothing beats this city in daylight, all shiny when the sun hits it right. But there is something about it in the nighttime too. A different energy. Plans are made in the day, but the night seems to be the time they play out. Despite everything, I can't help but notice the hope building in my chest.

'What do you think you want your art to say?' I ask Remi.

'I'm not sure yet,' she muses. 'What about you?'

'Well, I'm wondering if I should use it for the things I might not say otherwise.'

'Yes,' says Remi, 'I like that.' But she doesn't press and I like *that*.

Chapter Twenty

'Remi, thank you so much for having me at your place. Such a quick trip to get home,' I say as we walk from the train station to her house. When we feel the first few drops of summer rain we speed up.

'Of course,' says Remi, at a slow run now. 'It really didn't make sense for you to go home so late when I have an empty house.'

'Do you mind your family going on a trip without you?' I ask, keeping pace. When Remi told me her mum and little brother were away for the week without her, I couldn't believe it. There is no way my parents would leave me by myself for a week.

'I actually love it,' says Remi. 'I miss them, but I keep

busy and even though it's sometimes unnerving I like the quiet of the house.'

I nudge her with my elbow. 'Especially in the early hours of the morning, right?'

Remi laughs. 'You got it!' She unlocks the door and, as we walk in, she hangs her keys up on a hook by the door.

Remi motions to the shoes that sit in small cubbies next to the entrance. 'Do you mind taking your shoes off? I'll give you a pair of house shoes. What size are you?'

'Maybe about a six.'

She passes me a pair of open-toe slippers. 'Try these.'

I pull off my sandals and slide my slippers on.

Feet all cosy, I turn to Remi. 'Where shall I put my stuff and also where's your loo?' I ask.

'First door on the left is where you'll be tonight, and bathroom is the door opposite,' she says, opening both doors for me.

I dump my bag quickly in the bedroom without pausing to turn on the light, then head to the bathroom. I splash some water on my face, and it's not till I'm sitting on the toilet that I notice the poster on the back of the bathroom door.

For you created my inmost being;
you knit me together in my mother's womb.

I praise you because I am fearfully and wonderfully
made;
your works are wonderful,
I know that full well.
My frame was not hidden from you
when I was made in the secret place,
when I was woven together in the depths of the earth.
Your eyes saw my unformed body;
all the days ordained for me were written in your book
before one of them came to be.

After I wash my hands, I grab my phone from my pocket and take a photo of the poster.

Remi is stacking a couple of dishes in the dishwasher. 'Remi, what does that sign on the back of your door mean?' I ask. 'It's kind of beautiful. Is it talking about destiny?'

'Huh?' says Remi, looking up.

'You know, on the back of the toilet door?'

'Oh, that.' Remi laughs. 'I kind of forget it's there. Well, maybe not quite destiny, but more like a purpose. Our bodies, us, were made by God carefully, intricately with a plan and a purpose. It's from Psalm 139.'

I look at her blankly.

'From the Bible.'

'Oh, okay.' Neither of us speaks for a moment as I look at the words again.

'I didn't notice the God bit. But I do like the idea that we have been made for a purpose, even though I am a bit weird about plans.'

Remi nods. 'I love that verse. It gives me confidence, comfort, knowing that while I am deeply flawed, I exist for a reason, life isn't meaningless.'

'I didn't know you were so religious,' I say.

'I guess so,' says Remi. 'I like to think of myself as a person of faith, like I'm not just going through the motions. Don't you remember Lachlan asking us what we believed in, that day at the Art Gallery?'

I think back. 'Oh yeah, he did. You must have said yes.'

'I did,' says Remi. 'I didn't want to make a big fuss about it that day, but it's pretty important to me.'

'I guess I didn't take that much notice,' I say upon reflection. 'I was too busy trying to make my mind up about all the other questions. I hope you don't mind me keeping a photo of the back of your toilet door,' I say, attempting to make it seem less like I am interrogating her life decisions.

'I love that you want to keep it,' Remi says as her phone pings. She picks it up from the bench and looks at it.

'Oh,' she says. 'So that's Mattias.'

I sit up a bit straighter.

'He said that buses are replacing trains and the next one isn't coming for another hour.'

‘That sucks.’ I say. ‘The bus takes extra-long too.’

‘Should I tell him to just come here? What do you think?’

I shrug, trying to be casual. ‘It’s your house, if you don’t mind, I don’t mind. And you probably need to be like that guy who helps out his brother . . . or was it his neighbour, his friend?

‘Do you mean the good Samaritan?’

‘I think that’s the one I mean,’ I say, stretching my mind back to primary school scripture.

‘I don’t have to suggest he come here,’ says Remi. ‘If we want a girls’ night?’

My heart flips over a little. ‘It’s fine.’

‘Only if you’re sure?’

I give a firm nod. ‘Of course, you should help him out.’

Remi picks her phone back up, then placing it back down she looks at me. ‘Did you invite him to Bondi yet?’

‘No, I didn’t really get a chance, we didn’t speak yesterday.’

‘You didn’t message?’ she asks.

‘No,’ I say. ‘He hasn’t really sat with us these last couple of days. Last time we spoke we kinda got cut off, and it hasn’t been the same.’ It’s not the full story, but I’m not sure I want to explain it all. ‘You know what? It’s all good, I guess we can ask him tonight.’

'True,' Remi says with a nod. 'Hey, I should have asked this earlier, but do you mind being in my brother's room? He's got bunkbeds.'

'Sure,' I say.

'And would it be terrible if I asked you to share with Mattias?' she continues. 'I'm sorry to make it even weirder. I'd share with you and put him in my room, but if my Mum caught wind of there being a boy in my room, much less my bed, she wouldn't be happy.'

I feel my eyes widen. 'Um, I could take the couch?' I offer.

'You could try,' says Remi. 'But it is really uncomfortable; it's got this odd sag in the middle. Mum has been meaning to get a new one, but . . .' she trails off. 'It's really up to you.'

If my sister were here, we would have plotted out exactly what I should do and say. I would know exactly what needed to be done. Without her, I feel like I am floundering around in the dark. It's so hard to know what to do. Instead of making a decision, I suggest a cup of tea, and busy myself in Remi's kitchen finding and filling the kettle, then asking her where the mugs and tea bags are.

Remi and I are sitting on stools at the bench when we hear a knock on the front door. My stomach flips. I catch

Remi's eye and she smiles at me, nods as if telling me it's going to be okay. I stay in the kitchen and listen to Remi open the door and greet Mattias.

'Thank you, Remi,' he says. 'I'm so fed up with busses. I thought the trains would still be going, but we finished up later than I expected. And you had said you were happy to have people stay . . .' His voice trails off as his eyes flick around the house and land on me.

Remi, bless her, takes control of the situation. 'Absolutely, happy to have you stay. Cleo is here too, come say hi.' I shift on my stool, tea in hand, sitting up straighter while Mattias takes his shoes off.

When Mattias walks into the kitchen behind Remi, I see his hair is wet. He pushes it off his face then has to wipe his hand on his pants.

'Is it heavy out there now?' I ask.

'It's really coming down, I had to run the last fifty metres to the door.'

'I'll get you a towel,' says Remi.

Mattias and I look at each other for what feels like an hour but is probably only a few seconds. He doesn't speak. I give him a small, tight-lipped smile.

'Sorry to crash your time together,' Mattias finally says. 'I hadn't realised. But I am grateful, I didn't think I could handle the bus tonight.'

'It's fine,' I say with more conviction than I perhaps feel.

He turns to face me again and it looks like he's about to say something but then stops. I wonder when I became a person who catalogues the number of times someone looks at me. Then realise I've probably always done it, classic overthinker that I am.

Remi comes back out and tosses a towel to Mattias and while he rubs his hair with it, she hands me a pile of bed linen and a pillow.

'I've already let Cleo know, but Henry normally sleeps on the top so there are sheets on there, but whoever is on the bottom will need these.' The sheets are a light blue with a pattern of red and yellow diggers on them and a pillow.

'Riiiiiiight,' says Mattias drawing it out realising the subtext of Remi's comment, that we are going to be sharing a room. 'You know I'm honestly happy on the couch,' he says. 'Cleo probably wants her own space.' He looks at me as if waiting for me to confirm.

What he doesn't know, what I'm not going to say out loud, is that the thought of sharing a room feels equal parts terrifying and wonderful.

I shrug, trying out cool and casual for once. 'I don't mind. Also, Remi said the couch is really uncomfortable.'

There is a beat while Mattias takes the information in. He looks surprised but holds his hands out for the linen.

'Luckily, I'm super into construction. Excavators are probably my favourite of all the earth-moving machines,' he says taking the sheets, a wry smile on his face.

Remi's brother Henry's room is littered with signs of ten-year-old activity. From the Pokémon and Minecraft posters to the Ninjago Lego set, it's clear who this room belongs to.

'I'm exhausted,' says Remi. 'I think I'll turn in. Mattias, the bathroom is across the way and if you want another towel, there are plenty in the linen press. If you need anything else, let me know.' She gives my arm another squeeze and leaves us standing in the room.

With Remi gone, things go back to feeling strained.

'So, are you happy with the diggers on the bottom?' I ask as Mattias studies the Lego.

'Sure, if being on top suits you.' He doesn't realise what he has said until a moment later. He looks away and I am glad because I feel a blush creeping onto my face. I can't help but think if Lachlan were here, he would make a stupid joke – but to be honest I really don't want to think about Lachlan right now.

Not knowing what else to do, I offer Mattias help. 'Want a hand making the bed?'

'Thanks,' he says, then adds, 'but I think I've got it.'

The bunks are pushed into the corner, which makes the most of the space in the small room but also means making the bed is trickier than normal. Mattias stands at the end and flings the fitted sheet out towards the top. He starts tucking his end of the sheet under the mattress while I watch on. By the time he's walked round the ladder to tuck it in at the top, the bottom end has popped off.

He stands back and scratches his head. 'I spoke too soon. Cleo, please help me.'

He goes back to the bottom of the bed and I stand at the top left corner and stretch the cotton over the edge I can reach. Unfortunately, I don't have the wingspan to reach the other side. Because of the ladder, I can't pull the mattress off the bed and because of the walls, I can't walk around it.

'Damn,' I mutter, unsure of how to manage the situation. In the end, I climb onto the bed and pull the sheet up under me up to the top right corner. I'm all too aware that now I'm sitting where Mattias will sleep and also that making a bed with someone who is not your mum or your sister feels more intimate than I would have imagined. Even if it is a bunk bed with diggers on it.

Mattias hasn't said anything, but I feel that there is a question left unanswered between us and that it needs to be addressed. 'I don't want to talk about the phone,' I say.

'You don't have to,' says Mattias. He shakes the flat sheet and flings it across the bed. He swallows visibly and puts the pillowcase onto the pillow, then tosses it towards me. 'It's okay,' he says, but things don't feel okay.

I put the pillow in place, then spin my legs around back down to the floor.

He sits next to me before I can stand up.

We sit in silence.

I'd like to think I'm so chill, but inside my heart is beating and my voice catches when I speak.

'It's not really okay. I'm sorry.'

And I don't know why, but I don't move.

He stays there too, maybe he's worried that any sudden movement will freak me out, I don't know. But I appreciate his presence. 'Thanks, for not pushing,' I say before getting up and collecting my things to clean my teeth.

When I return to the bedroom, the light is already off and I can just make out Mattias in the bottom bunk.

Chapter Twenty-One

I lie on the top bunk. Every time Mattias moves I can hear him. The sheet's rustle or bed's creak.

After a while Mattias is still.

It's late but I can't sleep. I take my phone out of my pj pocket and begin to write a message to my sister that I know will never be read.

I wish there was a plan for what to say when you're sharing a room with the boy you like but you've made it clear you need space and have built a safety wall around yourself but what you've actually done is trapped yourself . . .

I send the message, sighing into the darkness.

'Who are you texting at this time of night?' Mattias's voice startles me and I almost drop my phone.

'I thought you were asleep.'

'Nope.'

'You were still.'

'Haha, despite that I'm *still* not asleep. Your texting isn't as quiet as you think it is, plus it takes me ages to fall asleep in new places, so no stress.'

'Me too. Sorry. I'll try to be quiet.'

'I don't mind,' he says. 'I'm happy to chat, but I don't want to . . .'

'Force me to share my most intimate thoughts?' I ask, for reasons that are unclear to me.

'What? No!' He sounds slightly horrified. 'I wasn't trying anything. I know that's not what you want.'

'Sorry, that was a dumb thing to say, I know you're not,' I say.

No one speaks and it's silent again.

'I missed working near you and chatting to you these last couple of days,' I admit.

'You can always talk to me,' he says.

And because it's dark and I'm tired and he speaks with such sincerity, I pull a couple of the bricks down. 'I'm so embarrassed,' I say, then chance it by taking a few more down. 'I'm sorry I messed up our hang out.' Mattias doesn't answer. 'I obviously panicked and it was such a fun day, but I think the moral of the story is, I'm not relationship material.'

Wow, that was bold, and not just because I implied he'd want a relationship with me. I mean, does he?

Mattias is quiet but I hear the sheets rustle.

'I'm glad the first part was fun,' he says.

Lying here, I want to tell him everything. But I can't, because things are still too raw and that is about 500 bricks too many to take away at once. But maybe I could tell him part of it.

'You remember how I said my sister used to make how-to-guides for me? Like, plans for life?'

'Yes?' His voice is soft.

'Well, I didn't tell you why she did that.' Mattias doesn't speak, and I take it to mean he is listening, so I continue dismantling the wall, brick by brick. 'Clearly, I'm not a tower of confidence. I'm a pretty anxious person; like, not diagnosed or anything, but when I was younger, I felt things even more acutely. New situations felt insurmountable and starting high school, was, well, hard. I would kind of spiral out? But my sister, it was like she always knew exactly what I needed, even when my mum didn't, even when I didn't. And we got into this habit of her writing me these plans, to help me to visualise, imagine and prepare for everything that was coming my way. It started as a coping mechanism but ended up as a way we'd connect,' I say, smiling at the memory of some of the funnier ones.

'What did you have plans for?' asks Mattias.

'Well, the first was for starting new things, particularly high school, which was super helpful. Then we had ones for making conversation, making friends, going to parties. They evolved over the years.' I deliberately don't mention first kisses. 'Anytime she learned or experienced something new, it was her way of both sharing it with me and preparing me. One time she made me a plan for buying Christmas presents.' A giggle busts out of me. 'It was totally self-serving, and very memorable.'

'She sounds pretty cool,' says Mattias.

'Yeah,' I say, and don't correct his tense, because in this moment it feels like she is still here and I don't want to lose it. 'Those plans really help me,' I say.

I hear Mattias shift in his bed. 'That's really special.'

I let the silence wrap around us. I can just make out Mattias breathing in a steady pattern.

'You know the exhibition we saw today?'

'Yeah?'

'It might not be the point of it, but do you think we have finite room in our lives?'

'Well, there's finite time, that's clear.'

'That's true, but I think I'm more asking about emotional space, relational space? Like, is there always room?'

'Do you mean like, can someone have too many friends?'

'Maybe?'

'I guess it comes back to the time thing. If we had infinite time, we could have an infinite number of friends and experiences, but because we don't maybe it's about choosing which relationships we want to hold on to.'

'That makes sense,' I say, even though I'm not sure I've gotten to the bottom of how I'm feeling.

I think for a moment.

'I would like to hold onto you and Remi and Lachlan. You know, after this program is finished. I hope we will still be friends.'

Now it's Mattias's turn to be silent.

'So . . .' says Mattias, after a moment, 'speaking of Lachlan, there's something I wanted to tell you.'

I wonder where this is going.

'You know how I told you about me switching sports?' Mattias asks.

'Yes,' I say, unsure how this is connected to Lachlan.

'Well, the truth is a little more detailed than I might have let on.'

I lie still, afraid to break the spell, that I might spook *him* if *I* ask too many questions.

'I was unlike you in year 6; I was excited for year 7. Keen to try new subjects, wanting to learn. I had friends from primary school going with me, but I was happy to meet new kids too.'

I nod silently in the dark, knowing Mattias can't see me but wanting to acknowledge what he is saying in some way.

'The first few months were great. It was an easy transition. Until we began a gymnastics unit in our PE class. I still remember that first lesson. I was pumped. I wasn't great at ball sports, not terrible mind you, but I would never have been picked first for a team. So, when I saw the mini trampoline and the parallel bars and tumbling strip set up for the lesson, I felt like finally I had this chance to show my friends what I was good at.'

'What colour was your sports shirt?' I ask, unable to stop myself.

'Sorry?'

'I'm just picturing you as a twelve-year-old in your PE gear but I realised I didn't know the colour of your uniform.'

'It's a tricolour type thing, red, white and green. Kinda Christmassy, actually,' he says, and I hear the smile in his voice. It makes me smile too.

'So, you're ready to mini tramp in your Christmas shirt . . .' I say.

'I think it wasn't the mini tramp that was the problem, it was the parallel bars.'

'Why was that the problem?'

'Because I called them the p-bars, because that's what we called them at gym and I was actually good at them and I guess Lachlan wasn't used to not being the best at a sport and so he started the name Pee-Pee-Matt-Tee.' Mattias gets it all out in one breath.

'Seriously? He was twelve and he called you that name?'

'Yep.'

'I mean, if he was five, I think it would make more sense,' I say, trying to imagine it. 'It's just so juvenile. But year 7 boys, I guess?'

'Yeah. Somehow the name stuck and I was called that or "gymspastic", which firstly, not okay to use that term as an insult, and as you can imagine made me feel amazing about myself.'

I hear the sarcasm in his voice. 'That's awful,' I say, rolling on to my side, resting my head on my hand.

'Lachlan left halfway through the year and the name was mostly forgotten, but my place in the pecking order remained unchanged. It didn't help that Dad left around the same time. I think I just put my head down from then on and did my best not to stand out. I also told my mum I didn't want to do gymnastics anymore.'

'Did she suggest the parkour or did you decide on that?' I ask, intrigued at how other families work.

'That was Mum. She said I couldn't just do nothing but I think she knew she couldn't push me into anything either. She started watching parkour shorts. She'd be watching it making all these noises, like "Oh wow!", and taking exaggerated intakes of breath like something was really intense, and of course she knew I'd want to know what she was watching. I'd come around and see it over her shoulder. It hooked me in right away because I thought, with my training, I could already do a bunch of the stuff those guys were doing. When Mum caught me flipping off the retaining wall out the back of my gran's house, she knew she had me. She booked me into a class at the same place where I used to do gym and I was set. I loved it. But I didn't really talk about it at school, and I knew not to show off because I didn't want the attention again. So, I just kept those two aspects of life separate, at-school Mattias and at-home Mattias.'

I'm not sure how to respond to what Mattias has told me. 'I'm sorry you had to go through all that,' I say. 'Thank you for trusting me enough to tell me.'

There's a silence between us, not awkward, more thoughtful and I start to connect some of the dots.

'Is that why you went to Lachlan's party that night? That makes sense now, why you two haven't really gelled. Oh gosh.' I groan, embarrassed now. 'And here I am thinking about what good friends we are, and what a great time we've had, when all along it's been tough for you. How self-centred am I?' I smack myself with my hand. Then, even though he can't see me, I put my pillow over my head. I feel like an idiot.

'Did you just facepalm?' Mattias asks.

'Yeah,' I say, my voice muffled by the pillow.

'What are you doing now?' he asks.

'Hiding my shame under my pillow.'

Mattias chuckles, then after a moment says, 'You know, you aren't entirely wrong . . .'

I peep out from the pillow. 'Yes?' My voice is a whisper and now I want to go down there and look at his face while he is talking to me, but I can't make myself do that.

He takes a breath. 'When I got invited to this class, I was excited. This was my chance, I thought, to not be that kid. The one who had been shamed at the start of high school, pigeonholed and put in a box. Not willing to show what he could do, who he could be. I wanted the opportunity, not to be someone else but to be seen for the first time as myself. Or if not myself, then the person I wanted to be.'

When Mattias pauses I affirm him. 'I get it. That makes sense.'

'I think I wanted to be more confident. To be the person who sees what he wants and goes after it. Which I did. Or I tried to, but that doesn't matter. But when I saw Lachlan, I thought that was it. I was right back in year 7 again, ready to be ridiculed. I felt uncomfortable again, like, uncomfortable in my skin. But I couldn't believe it, over the first few lessons, he didn't seem to remember me. And then when I went to the party, I didn't get to talk to him, but I did get to talk to you. So, I decided to put him out of my mind again and concentrate on the good things that were in front of me. And it's been so great hanging with you . . . and Remi.'

'I'm glad we met,' I say.

'Me too,' he says, and a shiver runs through me. He's actually easy to talk to. So real. Not the person I thought he was when we first met.

'For what it's worth,' I say, 'I think you achieved your goal.'

'What do you mean?'

'Okay, when we first met, I thought you were so cool, it was like you had everything together and you didn't need anyone or anything else. Remember, I told you I assumed you were the most popular person at your school.'

He chuckles.

I wonder for a moment if things can be different. I wonder if maybe it can be as simple as a girl liking a boy who likes her back. But there's not always room. And I can't do it. Instead, I say, 'We're friends now though, right? We're good, aren't we? Especially now I know you aren't super popular, I feel much more comfortable.'

'Sure,' he says. 'We're friends.'

'Hey, friend? Want to come to Bondi with us on the weekend? Full disclosure, Lachlan will be coming.'

'I think I can deal with that.'

'Night, friend,' I say.

'Night,' he replies, and I feel about three-quarters relief and one-quarter regret.

Chapter Twenty-Two

I wake and it takes me a moment to realise where I am. Then I remember that I'm at Remi's house, that I'm lying in her brother's room and that I was up late chatting to Mattias. It feels good. I listen to see if he's awake and realise I can't hear anything.

I wander into the kitchen and see Remi sitting at the bench munching on some toast. 'How'd you sleep?' she asks.

'Pretty good,' I say.

'You chat much?'

'A bit. You know, I invited him to Bondi, I think he might come.'

'Neat.'

'Where is he?'

'He left earlier, I think he wanted to go for a run or something? I can't understand it.'

'Oh,' I say, trying not to sound too disappointed to have missed him. Instead I focus on enjoying my time with Remi.

On the way to class, I ask Remi, 'When did you feel okay talking about your dad?'

'Oh, um, it happened when I was eight so I'm not sure there was ever a time when I didn't just tell people. I think it was more a problem that I'd just blurt out, "My dad is dead" in really inappropriate places. Like this one time, my year 3 teacher was telling us about parent–teacher interviews and I just put my hand up and was like, "It'll just be my mum this year, because my dad is dead." My teacher didn't know how to respond, but the other kids in my class already knew; they were like, yeah, it's old news. I mean, it was awful, but I never had to worry about how to tell people.' She pauses and turns to me. 'Why do you ask?' Her tone is light but when she sees my face she stops. 'Cleo, are you okay? Did you lose someone?'

Her no-nonsense question shakes the answer loose. 'My sister.'

'Was it recent?'

I sigh. 'Sometimes it feels like yesterday. But it was almost two years ago.'

'What was she like?' Remi's face is open, waiting for me to speak. It's a beautiful question.

I take a big breath and smile. 'She was almost the complete opposite of me. She was . . .' I search for the right words. 'Popular, school captain, netball star, academically gifted. Universally known and loved. I think that's been the weirdest thing about being here. I'm not used to people not knowing her,' I say. 'Everyone at my school knew her. Everyone in my life knew her. But it's been different here and I don't know if I like it or not.'

Remi nods but doesn't say anything.

'She's been such an important part of my life, perhaps the most important part. But when I'm with people who didn't know her, it makes me feel like I'm even further away from her, but then I also don't want to be the most pathetic sad girl, you know?'

'That's difficult, Cleo. Does it feel like you're moving on without her?'

'Yeah.' Remi has nailed it. It is so easy talking to her and it makes me wonder why I couldn't just tell Mattias last night. 'Do you ever feel like that?' I ask her. 'That you keep moving further away from your dad?'

'Sometimes I do. But I guess for me, if life had stopped there, when I was eight, that would have been even worse, you know. But Cleo, it's okay to feel your feelings. When my dad died, I thought I had to be okay all the time. For my mum, for my brother. But bottling it all up just made it worse.'

'So, what did you do?'

'Counselling,' says Remi, 'lots of it. It's why I'm so' – she makes quotation marks in the air – '"well adjusted".'

'My mum has a counsellor,' I say, 'but I don't like her that much.'

'Does your mum?'

'She loves her! Can't stop telling us about her. "Jean said this", "Jean thinks that". It's exhausting.'

'You know what, Cleo, I don't think your sister sounds all that different to you at all. In my experience you're universally known and loved too.'

'Remi, you are the ultimate hype woman,' I say with a laugh. We walk a bit further. 'Thank you, Remi,' I say, and I mean it.

'You know,' says Remi, dodging the other foot traffic, 'it's nice to talk about something that's real. It's fun choosing between hotdogs and hamburgers or whatever, but this' – she gestures between me and her – 'this is a real conversation and I appreciate it.'

'I appreciate you,' I say with a grin.

Our model for the day is Miia. Her limbs are elongated and she looks like a ballet dancer. Even though I have finally come to terms with the naked form, I seem to be having trouble in our warmups. I can't help thinking I should have told Mattias everything, like I did with Remi. I had the chance and I didn't take it. He is working next to me again and when I look at him, I want to smile, but I can't seem to get it together on the page today.

'Your strokes seem angry today,' says Betty, standing behind my work. 'They feel too tight, too constricted, like you want to let loose but haven't been able to. We need to find that freedom again.' It's true I've been frustrated with my two-minute sketches of Miia, and while I'm not sure if I can see the anger in my linework, I can certainly feel it in my heart.

Betty brings small pots half full of black liquid and paintbrushes around to us. Next, she brings jars of clean water. 'Something new,' she says. 'We will take up our two-minute sketches of Miia again. This time we will be working with inks. Anyone worked with inks before?' No one raises a hand. 'Okay, class, if you want to make your way over to my easel.' She waits while we file over to her and then fan out behind her. 'I'll give a demonstration.'

Betty wets her brush in the water, then dips it into the ink. 'There are a number of different ways to do this, but I like to begin with only a small amount of ink on my brush. Keep it quite pale in colour as we block out the shape Miia is holding. You see?' she asks, turning around and waiting for us to respond. 'Good. Next, load up your brush again. Now we want enough ink for a nice solid line, but not too much so that it drips everywhere.' She pauses. 'Unless that is the look you are going for.'

Betty dips her brush into the ink again and dabs it on the side of the jar. 'Now with this, we are aiming for speed and confidence. You have the shape already there, so now with only a few lines – and less IS more here, people – you will draw the body.' Betty looks up at Miia, then commits what she sees to the page in four strokes. The result is stunning and I can't wait to give it a try.

Before we leave for the day, Mattias comes over. 'See you on Saturday, right?'

'Yep, at the markets, just call if you can't find us,' I say, heart squeezing in anticipation.

Chapter Twenty-three

'I can't believe you've never been to Bondi before.' Remi nudges me with her shoulder, motioning to the button we need to press to inform the driver that we will get off at the next stop.

'*I* can't believe I've never been to Bondi before, Remi,' I say, reaching for the red button and pressing it.

Remi starts to stand and I do the same. I step into the bus aisle and swing my overstuffed bag on my back. 'Manly, yes. Wollongong, of course. North Gong? Bulli? Further south? Jervis?' I count the Sydney and South Coast beaches off my fingers. 'But Bondi? Only the most well-known beach in Australia? Never in my life.' We step off the bus. 'I'm not really sure why, but I recognise it's weird.'

Remi has told me the markets are at Bondi Beach Public School, at the north end of the beach. Although the beach is on the other side of the road, I can see the water stretching to the horizon. I'm looking forward to feeling the sand between my toes, but I'm not sure how I feel about fighting for that patch of sand. People are everywhere.

Before we step into the fray across the road, Remi leads me towards the market gates. One of the buildings at the edge of the school has a giant mural. The beach is depicted in portrait, stretching up to the sky. A small child writes the word 'peace' in the sand and around him are panels of patterns.

'The peace mural,' Remi says. 'I can't remember when they did it, but maybe thirty-odd years ago? The panels around the sides were done by the children attending the school at the time. They are supposed to represent all their different cultures coming together. Pretty neat.'

We are standing looking at the mural when I feel an arm around my shoulders. I smother my startle reflex. It's Lachlan.

'What are we thinking about, ladies?' He pauses for a moment before answering his own question. 'World peace?' he asks, adopting the false high-pitched tone of a beauty pageant contestant.

'Urgh, Lachlan,' says Remi, shrugging off his arm.

'Okay, serious question then,' he says, changing tack. 'What's the thing you want the most? What word would you write in the sand?'

Sometimes Lachlan feels like too much, but he is good at getting a conversation going. What *would* I wish for?

'Come on, Cleo, you can think of something,' Lachlan says.

I'm still thinking when Remi replies. 'Equity,' she says and I nod in agreement before answering.

'I know I should say clean water for all or the end to poverty, and yes, I can count, they are not one-word answers, but for me, maybe . . .' I scrunch up my face before answering. I am so pathetic. 'Assurance.' I just want to trust myself, not second guess everything. 'That's what I would ask for.'

A second later I realise that, ironically, that is not it at all. 'Resurrection,' I say.

'What?' asks Lachlan.

'I'd want my sister back,' I say, and Remi reaches over and gives me a quick hug.

'Oh,' says Lachlan, reading between the lines. 'Sure.' Then he adds, 'Well, you know, not to shift the mood too much, and obviously not of equal importance, but my word would be food.' I roll my eyes. 'I am stinging for some gozleme,' he says, his face cracking wide open in a massive smile.

'You are the worst,' says Remi.

'Or the best?' asks Lachlan.

'Perhaps somewhere in between,' I answer and we head into the markets in search of food and inspiration.

The gozleme is hot and I lick the sour tang of lemon off my fingers before taking a bite of spinach and feta sandwiched between thin dough.

'Pretty good, right?' asks Lachlan.

My mouth is full and I let out a satisfied sigh of agreement while Remi nods her head. The sun heats my back and I take a couple of sips of water before squeezing more lemon onto my lunch.

'Hey, did you girls invite Mattias?' asks Lachlan between mouthfuls. 'Because that looks like him over there.'

I look up. I don't think he can see us. He wears the same black board shorts he wore during our beach day and a light grey t-shirt. A dark green cap sits on his head. I feel instantly both nervous and excited.

'I did,' I say. 'Felt like he was one of us now.'

'Sure thing.' Lachlan's words sound more welcoming than his tone, making me wonder if he does actually remember Mattias from five years ago.

I lift my hand and wave until Mattias notices, my head cocked to one side. I see a smile slide on to his face when he spies us.

'Hey,' he says by way of greeting, giving Lachlan a gentle clap on the back and Remi, then me, a quick side hug. He handles the greeting so naturally that I am momentarily jealous of his calm. It sits in strong contrast to the jittery way I said hello to him when I visited his house.

'No handshake?' I ask. I want to remind him that we had something, that there was something that existed between us outside of the others.

'A handshake?' questions Lachlan, his eyebrows wiggling, looking between his suggestively. 'What's this?'

Now I'm embarrassed and weirdly exposed and wish I hadn't brought it up. 'It's nothing,' I say, ignoring how I feel and adopting Mattias's attitude.

But it's like Lachlan has found a sore and wants to pick at it for a while. 'Go on, you two, why are you shaking hands? Is this a job interview? Or is it your secret handshake? I know, it's for a secret club. I want to be part of your club. Show it to me. *Teach* it to me!'

Lachlan is normally so friendly, so fun in a group setting, but this doesn't feel fun anymore and I don't know what to say or do.

Remi looks between us, picking up on the off vibes. 'Hey, didn't you want to check out those printed tea towels I was telling you about?' she asks, attempting to pull us out of this stalemate.

My brain springs into action. 'Yes,' I say. 'Yes, I do.' I vaguely remember Remi mentioned something about tea towels with animal prints. They felt like something my mum would like, but right now in this moment I think I would like them very much. Remi points over her right shoulder and I turn in that direction, but stop when I hear Mattias.

His voice is friendly yet firm. 'If I showed you it wouldn't be secret anymore, now would it? I'm sorry but you'll have to find your own club.'

Lachlan nods, contrite. 'Fair enough, a gentleman never tells,' he says, making the whole thing worse.

I turn towards the tea towels. 'Think I'll get my mum a present,' I say, and walk away from the boys.

Remi walks next to me. 'So, I know asking this puts me in danger of not passing the Bechdel test,' she begins.

'The Bechdal test?'

'The Bech*del* test,' Remi corrects. 'You haven't heard of it?'

I shake my head.

'It's a way of testing the representation of women in films. Like, if they are real characters or if they exist just to prop up the males in the film.'

'Okay,' I say.

'So, the test goes like this: if female characters only have conversations with male characters or if their conversations with other females revolve only around the male character, then the film fails the test. So, there have to be at least two or more women who talk about things other than men in the film.'

'That doesn't sound that hard to pass,' I say.

'You'd be surprised,' Remi answers. 'I think filmmakers these days are more conscious of representation, but yeah, there's way more than you would think that don't pass.'

'I'll be googling that tonight.' I pause. 'Sorry, why are we talking about the Bechdel test?'

'Well, I want to ask you what the heck is going on with you and those two?' Remi motions towards Mattias and Lachlan, who are looking at clay mugs and Dutch pancakes respectively.

'I know the answer to that,' I say. 'I haven't seen them like this before either but did you know they went to school together in year 7? You should ask Mattias exactly what happened.' I don't want to give away what he has trusted me with. 'Let's just say, they weren't particularly tight.'

'That rings true. He doesn't seem to like Lachlan that much.'

I'm looking at some silky-feeling kimono-type robes. The patterns are bright and bold. I hold up a purple one with large flowers and Remi points towards a turquoise one with a smaller, more geometric print. She's right, it suits me more.

'What about you?' asks Remi.

'Me?'

'Yes, you. Do you like Lachlan?'

I feel like squirming. This is the sort of conversation I would have with my sister, and only my sister, although these days Remi I feel closer and closer.

'Yes,' I say, then quickly add, 'I like Lachlan as a friend. In a "let's go to the beach with all our other friends together" sort of way.'

'Not in a "let's roll around in the sand just the two of us" kind of way?'

'Remi! No.'

We move on to the next stall. They stock a number of flowy dresses and blouses.

'What about Mattias?' she asks. 'Would you roll around in the sand with him?'

'Remi! What is it with you and rolling in the sand? And where are these questions coming from?'

'You're deflecting,' Remi says, giving me a pointed stare, before looking back at the shirts on the rack. 'Clearly there's a vibe going on. There has been all week.'

I find one a white one with a high neck and lace detail around the sleeves. I pull it out to get a better look.

'Do *you* want to roll around in the sand with either of them?' I ask, continuing to deflect.

'Absolutely not,' says Remi. 'My mother would kill me, and they're not my type. Also, you know, the fact you've not answered the question I think has answered my question.' She raises her eyebrow at me as if daring me to prove her wrong, then holds up a navy batwing-sleeved blouse with a mustard and white print on it. 'Can I try this one on?' she asks the stallholder.

I am left staring at the lace blouse and thinking about Mattias and the fact that I have so clearly defined our relationship as a friendship.

Do I want to roll around in the sand with him? I know I don't want to with Lachlan.

I think about Mattias's broad shoulders, his normally serious expression and the goofy look he gets when he allows himself to relax. I think about the way he's shared his past with me, the way he trusted me. Then I think about his fingers entwined in mine, our legs on the pool's edge and how I felt in the moments before my alarm went off, when it seemed like he was all that mattered in the world, when all I wanted was to feel his lips on mine, his mouth parted slightly, his tongue –

'Do you like it?' Remi's question snaps me out of my daydream and it takes me a moment to realise she is talking about the blouse and not anything or anyone else.

'Suits you,' I say. 'Are you going to get it?'

'You know what, I think I will,' she says, pulling out her wallet. 'Did you want to try that one on?'

'Nah, that's okay,' I say, then immediately feel disappointed in myself for not making a spontaneous shopping decision.

Mattias ambles over from the stall he has been looking at. 'Anything tickle your fancy?' I ask, sounding like my grandmother.

'A couple of things,' he says, but doesn't elaborate. A buzzer sounds inside my head. Eeeeh! Wrong answer, what I wanted him to say was, *'You, Cleo. You tickle my fancy.'* Or maybe not. I don't know how I would handle it.

Lachlan wanders over. 'You all ready to blow this joint? I need to get in the water.'

I can feel the heat of the midday sun on my back. I look at Remi for confirmation that she's seen enough. 'Let's head to the north end,' Remi suggests. 'It makes getting the bus back easier.'

'To the beach,' I say.

After we cross the road, Remi and I duck into the change-rooms to slip into our swimmers. I put my dress back on over my bikini; I'm not quite ready to shed every layer yet, despite all the nakedness I have seen over the past couple of weeks.

When Remi and I come out, we can't see the boys. 'Did they really not wait for us?' I ask.

We walk down towards the sand to look round. We look up and back and I'm about to give up when Remi says, 'Found 'em,' pointing towards some outdoor gym equipment.

Amidst a handful of die-hard exercise enthusiasts, we find Lachlan hanging from the highest bar. It's got to be over thirty degrees and there Lachlan is doing pull-ups. With his shirt off.

'Seven,' he counts, muscles contracting as he pulls up again. 'Eight . . . nine.' He slips a little, then re-grips. His elbows bend as he pulls himself to the bar, not fully making it, then straighten again as he drops down to the ground. He circles his shoulders, then shakes his arms out. I've got to admit, my initial impression of Lachlan was not wrong. With his shirt off, he does look like he can bench press me.

'Your turn, Mattias, let's see what you've got,' he says.

It's then that I realise what we've walked into is essentially a pissing match.

Mattias shakes his head; his expression reads like he can't believe Lachlan talked him into this. But then he reaches his right arm up and pulls his shirt up and off from the back collar. It's all I can do to keep my mouth closed.

Mattias is built in a different way to Lachlan. He is just as broad, but taller, leaner. His abs and his pecs are clearly defined yet seem somehow smoother. I can imagine running my hand over his chest and . . .

Remi notices me staring. 'You've got a little something here,' Remi says quietly so the boys can't hear, motioning at the corner of her lips.

'Huh?'

'A little drool maybe?' she suggests, a teasing smile playing on her face.

I dig my elbow into her ribs. 'Remi!'

'Need my towel to mop it up?' she says, motioning to her beach towel in her bag.

'Hardy ha ha,' I say, and hold my water bottle up to my cheeks to cool the flush that has begun to spread. I turn my attention back to Mattias.

He gives his arms a quick stretch, crossing one in front of his body, then elbow up to the sky.

'What do you think this is? A physie comp?' sledges Lachlan.

'Watch your mouth, Lachlan,' Remi says. 'Physie girls are fit, don't let them catch you talking like that.'

Finally ready, Mattias stands under the bar, then jumps to take hold of it. His legs bend slightly and he crosses his ankles neatly. His biceps flex as he pulls his chin to the bar.

'One,' calls Lachlan.

Mattias smoothly lowers himself down and, in what seems to be an effortless motion pulls his chin above the bar again.

'Two,' counts Lachlan. Then, 'Three, four, five.'

Remi and I join in the count. 'Six, seven, eight.'

Where Lachlan had slowed down by eight, Mattias looks like he is gaining speed. 'Nine.'

Mattias has easily matched Lachlan's total. On ten, rather than lowering back to the bar he pulls not just his chin to the bar but also his chest, then pushes up so his waist is at the bar. He leans his shoulders forwards and follows them with his torso, circling his whole body around the bar until he is in a hanging position again. Thinking he's finished, Lachlan starts to slow-clap him, but still Mattias doesn't drop down. He brings his knees up into a tuck in front of him and his toes go up to the bar. He tucks his toes and then his legs into the gap between his arms and the bar, almost like threading a needle. He tilts his butt so it faces up and lowers his legs so his toes point towards the ground. It's an impressive act of strength and control.

'Well now you're just showing off!' says Lachlan, looking a bit over the whole thing.

'But we love it,' says Remi, elbowing me. 'Don't we, Cleo.'

I'm so impressed I don't know what to say. I assumed Mattias was strong but seeing him in action is something else. 'Yes . . .' is all I manage to get out.

Mattias brings his legs back up from pointing down so they are horizontal again, then straightens his hips so that his whole body, apart from his arms, is in one line, pointing in the opposite direction to the way his fingers are facing. My phone is in my pocket and I quickly pull it out and snap a shot while he holds the position. He then brings his body into a tuck again, threads his legs back through the gap between his head and the bar and drops himself effortlessly onto the ground again.

Mattias looks straight at me and I smile at him in disbelief. 'That was amazing,' I tell him.

Lachlan shakes his head. I wonder what he will say, given the weird vibes between them earlier in the day. 'Feel like you played me, but well done, sir.' He slaps Mattias on the back. 'You know, if I could do that, it wouldn't be some secret skill; everyone would know about it.'

'That tracks,' says Remi, making me giggle. 'Now to the beach.'

Chapter Twenty-Four

I think I've always known that Emmy's 'Plans' were not just her way of helping me prepare for things as much as possible. They were also her way of connecting with me, her way of sharing something that she had learnt or experienced. I'm not sure when I realised that sometimes they were more about her than they were about me, but when she had her first kiss, I knew it was her way of including me in her experience. I was working on some maths homework when she opened the front door. I could tell she was elated.

'I'm writing a new guide,' she said, cheeks flushed pink. 'Come to my room in fifteen minutes and we can go through it.'

I was pleased. It provided an excellent excuse to take a homework break, and I felt like I hadn't properly spoken to Emmy in a couple of weeks, since she had started dating Anthony Chan.

Up until this point, Emmy had only even gone on group dates. The kind of outings someone organises because they think you are more likely to say yes to going out with a bunch of people. Emmy was notorious for saying no to potential suitors, so the fact she said yes to Anthony meant something. (On the other hand, I had been on zero dates, group dates included. My friendship circle wasn't one people easily mixed with.)

Emmy hadn't decorated the paper when she gave it to me. She hadn't had time.

When I read the title, I squealed in excitement.

'Was it Anthony?' I asked, making myself comfortable on her bed.

'Yes, I really like him,' she answered, grabbing her pillow and hugging it close to her. Her face was tinged pink and her smile remained. 'It was perfect.'

And she was quiet, giving me time to read her guide.

Plan For First Kisses

By Emmaline Markson for Cleo Markson

1. *Find the right partner. Your first kiss should be with someone you like and respect. It'll be more memorable if the person means something to you.*
2. *Setting is important. You do not want your first kiss to be in front of your friends or, even worse, his friends. You don't*

need more reasons to be embarrassed. It needs to be semi-private, but you want others close by in case things get out of hand.

3. *Eye contact is essential at the start. Maintained eye contact sends the message that you are interested and open for whatever might happen. Inability to look your partner in the eye means you are not sure and they shouldn't attempt it.*
4. *Physical contact is helpful. Before your lips touch, it may be good for another part of your body to be touching. (Get your head out of the gutter.) Maybe he will touch your cheek. Brush a strand of hair out of your face. Perhaps your hand will rest on his shoulder. Or his on the small of your back. All are good options and can increase the romance.*
5. *Lean in. This also signals to him that you are ready.*
6. *Close your eyes. (Or not. But eyes open can be a bit weird.)*

'Where were you?' I asked. She was so specific in her list about location, it made me wonder.

'Out the front of our house; he was saying goodbye. I know a front doorstep kiss is so cliche, but . . .' That's when she sighed. A big happy sigh. 'It was perfect. So romantic. Everything a first kiss should be.' She looked at me and I nodded, silently urging her for more details. 'The sun was starting to go down. You know that perfect afternoon timing where everything feels beautiful?'

She'd had a thing about twilight since she started playing around with photography. Everyone who knew her knew this was *her favourite time of day. I remember a part of me wondering how many times she might have mentioned this to Anthony, but discarding the thought almost as quickly as it came because I was so keen for more details.*

'And look at our jacaranda tree, the flowers are starting to coat the yard. It was magical. Now every time I see a jacaranda tree, I'll remember my first kiss.'

Despite the fact that I thought jacaranda trees were our thing, I smiled at her as she threw her pillow to me, like she was passing the baton on to me. 'You'll have your first kiss one day too, and it'll be just as magical.' She sounded so confident that I naively believed her. I held on to her belief.

The beach is heaving. There are people and towels dotted all along the sand. Children dig channels just past the shoreline, running in and out of the shallows to fill buckets with water.

I take my thongs off as we get to the sand, but with the sun at its highest my feet sizzle. I slide my shoes back on and notice the others doing the same.

Women and men alike are sunbaking, roasting their skin. There are families huddled in beach huts, snacking on Shapes and esky-cooled cans of drink. Teenagers older and younger than us parade along the waterfront, bodies on full display. A group of tanned men in tiny swimmer bottoms play keepie uppie with a soccer ball – no hands allowed.

We find a small pocket of sand only ten metres from the red and yellow flags. Someone must have just vacated it. We rummage in our bags for towels, fling them out and settle ourselves.

'I can't wait to get in the water,' I say, and grab my SPF out of my bag. 'Remi, are you able to sunscreen me?'

While Remi rubs the cream all over my back and into my shoulders, Lachlan hands his over and stands in front of me. I honestly don't think I've ever put sunscreen on anyone outside my family, and there's an intimacy to it that I hadn't realised before. I knew the curves and angles of my sister's shoulders and back, and I know where the straps of my mum's swimmers sit and the scar just to the right of my dad's spine. So it's totally weird to be rubbing cream on someone whose body I am unfamiliar with.

'Thank you, Remi,' I say, recognising it might be slightly weird for her too.

I'm working my way down to Lachlan's lower back when I look up and catch Mattias looking at me. I wish I knew what he was thinking.

I feel Remi squeeze my waist a tiny bit, egging me on. She noticed the look. 'Do you want me to do yours too?' I ask Mattias.

'Nah, that's alright.' Mattias pulls a Quiksilver rashie out of his bag and puts it on. 'I get cold in the water, it's a thermal one,' he says by way of explanation. 'Also cuts down on sunscreen.'

'Cool,' I reply, because what else can I say? Definitely not, *I really wanted my hands to be all over your perfectly muscled back, but that's okay, you do you.* No. That sentence is not coming out of my mouth, nor should I even be thinking it. Instead, I tell Lachlan that he is all done and ask Remi if I should do her back.

We sit on our towels, letting the sunscreen settle into our skin before heading into the water, warming our bodies so the cool of the water will be so much more enjoyable. 'Just fifteen minutes,' says Lachlan. 'I can't wait any longer than that.'

I should enjoy the time to relax but I feel self-conscious about the stretch marks on my thighs and I keep looking at my watch. At twelve minutes I can't stand it any longer. 'That's it,' I say, standing up. 'I'm going in.'

'Oh, thank goodness,' says Lachlan. 'Surely putting the cream on in the first place is the most important thing.'

'At this point I just want to get in the water,' I say.

The conditions are perfect. The waves are small and smooth. The water isn't churned up or at all sandy, and there's no seaweed to speak of. As we stride in, I turn to the side to jump each wave, and when I am waist-deep,

I dive under the next wave, opening my eyes as my sister and I always did to test the clarity of the water. 'It's so clear!' I cry upon resurfacing.

As I stand I realise I can see my feet through the water. A tiny sigh escapes me. It is beautiful.

Remi floats on her back between sets. 'Go on,' she urges me. 'Talk to him.'

And I really want to, but is there any point?

Remi nods at me. If she were any closer, she'd be elbowing me in my ribs urging me onwards, I swim closer to Mattias, diving into the water just before getting to him, then popping up next to him. 'Hi,' I say.

'Hi yourself,' he says, a smile forming on his face.

'Those were some pretty impressive moves just now.'

'Oh yeah?'

'You know they were,' I say, and he raises his eyebrows. 'Although I'm not sure it won you any favours with Lachlan.'

Mattias lifts his hands out of the water into a big, exaggerated shrug. 'Yet here we all are,' he says.

'Here we all are,' I repeat. 'Do you think there's a chance you will ever be friends?' Friendship is obviously on my brain.

'I'm trying,' he says. 'But I think we will need to at least acknowledge the past. And an apology would be nice.'

I mull over those words as we float over the peak of the next wave together. 'You know how I said that I find starting new things difficult?' I say. 'I've really enjoyed this time these holidays, and I –' I'm cut off by the next wave that comes. It's already broken and we dive underneath to avoid being pulled back in towards the shore.

Mattias surfaces seconds after me. 'And you . . .' he prompts.

'And I'm trying to work out how not to lose it all once school goes back.'

'Okay.'

'You know, finite time and all that. But I don't want to not see you.'

'You don't?' he asks.

'No . . . I was thinking about the time I visited you.'

'What about it?'

The moment you almost kissed me. I always think of that.

Nope.

That thought isn't helping anyone.

'That maybe I could come again? A redo?'

I let the water take my weight as we jump over the next wave. Mattias gestures to Lachlan, who is slightly closer to the shore than us and attempting to position himself just in front of the waves as they are about to break, ready to catch them all the way in. 'What I admire but also kind of hate about Lachlan is that he just goes for what he wants. Almost like he doesn't need to think about it and he doesn't care if there might be complications.'

'Yeah,' I agree, wondering where this is going and how it connects to what I said.

'I think because it's him it frustrates me more, but sometimes I wish I was like that.'

'Well, what would you just go for if you weren't complicating things?'

I watch him process the question. He keeps his eyes ahead, not looking at me. When he answers, it's not the answer I was expecting.

'Under,' he says, and I am confused.

'What?' I ask.

I realise what he is talking about a moment too late as Mattias dives under the next wave. This one is bigger than the last and has already broken. It takes me by surprise, pummelling me, pushing me back, holding me under before spitting me back up. I resurface and cough up the water I have swallowed. My dad always told my sister and me when we were kids not to turn our back on the ocean. 'Don't look away; she may be beautiful but she's unpredictable,' he'd say.

'Much like me,' Emmy would sometimes answer, splashing us all, which ironically became more and more predictable every time she said it.

Water has gone up my nose as well as getting into my mouth, and I attempt to discreetly blow my nose into my hand to get the excess ocean out and decrease the weird sensation. As I am rinsing off my hand, I hear a voice calling my name.

'Cleo! Cleo! Are you alright?'

Lachlan.

He wades over and places a gentle hand on my shoulder. 'Looks like you swallowed a bit of water. Getting dumped sucks, hey? I was thinking of heading in.' He cocks his head to the side. 'Want to come?'

My emotions are mixed. I'm annoyed that my conversation with Mattias was interrupted. I look for Mattias and finally clock him.

'Okay?' he calls out to me.

'I'll take her in,' Lachlan shouts back across the waves for me.

I'm feeling a little shaken and I'm upset with myself for getting distracted, not to mention embarrassed, so I throw Mattias a quick thumbs up and when Lachlan touches the small of my back, directing me towards the shore, I walk with him.

Lachlan flops straight onto his towel. I hover above mine, taking a moment to breathe. 'Do you ever just want to air-dry so your towel doesn't get too wet?' I ask.

'No,' says Lachlan. 'Never. Pretty sure that's what the towel is there for.'

I kind of don't want to lie straight down, but I know I'm being a bit stupid so I carefully kneel and then lower myself onto my stomach to at least keep some of the sand off my towel.

I sigh, put my sunglasses and hat on, then take out my water bottle and have a big drink.

The sun begins to reheat my skin and the saltwater dries on my face, crystallising around my eyes.

'Have you had a good summer?' Lachlan asks me.

I don't answer straight away.

'It's not the summer I thought it'd be,' I say after mulling it over. 'But you know, I'm pretty proud of myself for trying new things. How 'bout you?'

'It's had its moments,' Lachlan answers. He rolls over so he's facing me and props himself up on his elbow. When Lachlan speaks to you, he has a way of giving you all his attention. His eye contact says, *You're important. I'm interested.* But the moment suddenly feels too intimate and I'm uncomfortable.

I sit up. He follows suit.

'You know, there is one new thing that I've been wanting to try.'

In the distance, I see Mattias and Remi walking up the sand towards us. I feel relieved. I look back at Lachlan. 'Sorry, what did you want to try?'

Lachlan chuckles then looks serious again. 'No worries. Just this.'

All at once his hand is on my shoulder. And then . . .

Chapter Twenty-Five

Lachlan's tongue is in my mouth and I don't even know how this happened. Did I give him the impression that I wanted this? I don't want this.

I push Lachlan away and stand up, backing away from him.

Lachlan stands too, a bewildered look on his face.

Remi and Mattias are closer now and Mattias has broken into a run, his eyes locked on me.

He strides up to us and in one movement shoves Lachlan back onto the sand.

'This is exactly what I was talking about,' Mattias says, almost to himself. He directs his next sentence to Lachlan: 'You only think about yourself and taking what you want.'

Mattias is breathing deeply, clenching and unclenching his fists. He turns to me. 'Cleo, are you okay?' he asks.

I want to nod to tell him I'm okay, that I will be okay, but I'm frozen.

And I don't . . . I can't . . . I just . . . It's not . . . That's not . . . It wasn't . . .

I've been dumped again. I'm under water and I can't find the right way up. There's no air and none of my words can get to the surface.

I'm desperately trying to decipher the blur that just played out. As if someone took the remote and hit fast forward and only now have I got it back and pushed pause.

That was my first kiss.

My first kiss was stolen from me.

Taken in front of an audience.

I feel humiliated and exposed.

And no one says anything.

The wave is threatening to close in again and before the air leaves me, I look at Lachlan.

'I didn't want that,' I say, my voice cracking, my hands beginning to tremble. 'I didn't want to kiss you. Why did you do that?'

Mattias picks up my towel and wraps it around my shoulders.

Remi squeezes me in a hug.

Mattias looks at Lachlan, disdain blanketing his face. 'You need to go,' he tells Lachlan.

Lachlan looks confused, as if he wasn't the instigator, the lead role, the main character in this disastrous scene. 'I was just having some fun. You were having fun, right, Cleo? We were talking about trying new things.' He genuinely looks like he doesn't understand the effect he's had.

Remi doesn't buy it; she doesn't let him off the hook. 'You should always ask,' she says and there is an edge to her voice that I haven't heard before.

'I thought I was reading the situation,' says Lachlan. 'Cleo, I'm sorry, I thought you were into it.' It's like he can't contemplate someone not being interested.

'Lachlan, that's just it, that's why you need to ask. Because sometimes people read the situation wrong. It happens.' She picks his bag up and gives it to him. 'I think we need some space. We'll see you on Monday.'

Remi speaks like she is Lachlan's mother. Firm but fair. She reminds me of my sister, and I feel my eyes prickle, my chin wobble.

'Alright, I'll go, but is this because your sister is dead? Like, are you just super sad and abstaining from fun?'

A flick switches inside me, the shock is gone and anger takes its place.

'What did you say? What the actual . . .?'

It's all I can do not to scream at him, and the only reason I'm not doing that is because there are people all around us and I'm trying to hold onto the tiny shred of dignity I have left. I may not be shouting, but the edges of my words are sharp and I spit them at him.

'How dare you, you absolute shit of a person. First you take something from me, something you didn't ask for, something you just assumed I wanted, and then you try to make out that it's my fault? That the only reason I wouldn't like you is because I'm too sad? Screw you. I thought you were my friend. Just go.'

Lachlan has the decency to look surprised. He picks up his things and walks away.

I feel like I've gone a round in the ring, adrenaline now coursing through me.

Mattias looks at me and I can't read his expression. 'I didn't know your sister was dead,' he says, his voice soft, and I realise he's hurt. He's hurt I didn't tell him when Lachlan knew.

But I don't have any room for his pain and I don't owe him.

'I don't have to tell you anything,' I say, my voice softer in volume but still cutting.

'No, I know that,' he says. 'Actually, you know, I think I might head off too, it's probably for the best.'

'Good,' I say, not entirely sure what I mean.

'See you,' he says, and I don't reply.

Out of the corner of my eye I see Remi mouth 'sorry' to Mattias. Then she grabs my water bottle and tries to hand it to me. 'Maybe you'd like a drink?'

'No!' I say, because the anger is still there and it has to go somewhere. 'I don't want a drink. And you can stop trying to take care of me. You're not my sister.'

'I'm sorry,' she says, and gathers her things without another word.

When they've all gone, I sink down onto the sand and pull my towel tight around my shoulders.

Chapter Twenty-Six

I freaking hate catching buses.

This is something I should have remembered before picking a fight with all of my friends.

I have waited, like an idiot, for them to be far enough ahead of me so I don't have to face them on the bus back to the Junction, but now I realise my mistake. I don't know exactly where I am supposed to be catching the bus from. A tension headache pulls across my scalp and I pick myself up. It really would have made more sense to push my friends away once I was standing at the correct platform of the train station knowing how to get home.

What a spectacularly crap end to the day.

I GPS my way to a bus stop. Then sweat all the way to the Junction.

Trains are okay. Trains literally tell you what stop comes next, they prepare you and then, in case you missed it, each station is clearly labelled so you know when to get off. But buses? To a new destination? They suck. You are somehow expected to know exactly what where you are going looks like and not just that, but you need to know what the stop before it looks like so you can hit the button to let the driver know when to stop. And too bad if the bus is packed and you can't see out the window because people are standing down the aisle and you are in a stupid seat that isn't facing forward, or if the bus's advertising is blocking your view. Busses are a perfect metaphor for why I hate new things, because how the heck are you supposed to prepare for something you have nowhere near enough information about?

I keep my GPS running so I know when I get there. I want to feel angry at Remi all over again for leaving me but I'm so focused on the bus route on my phone that I have no room for other emotions.

When I finally get on the train I am depleted. Empty and exhausted, I sit in silence. Then my phone sounds. It's four o'clock. But I'm too tired to even draw on a memory so I just message her phone.

I had my first kiss today. It was spectacularly bad. Well, at least the circumstances were. It WAS NOT with a person I wanted to kiss. It was in public. And it WAS in front of the person I did want to kiss. And then I lost my shit, which I think you might have been proud of, but I kept losing it, which you wouldn't have liked so much. I wish you were here. I really need to talk to you about it.

I press send.

The train's aircon is out of control. I take my towel out and wrap it around me, wishing it was completely dry.

The house is quiet when I get home. Mum and Dad have gone to the movies, so the note on the bench says. How old-school. I head straight to the bathroom to wash the day off. In the shower, I let myself break down. Big, loud, ugly cries I only feel comfortable doing because Mum and Dad are out. I cry because I wanted my first kiss to be a beautiful memory and now it is tarnished forever. I cry because I've pushed Remi away just as I was letting her in. I cry because even though it was never going to happen with Mattias I was still enjoying the tingles of possibility. I cry because I NEED my sister. I cry because I don't know what to do and because somehow I have to face them all again on Monday.

I'm in bed playing 'Graffiti' by Chvrches on repeat when I get a message. It's from Mattias.

I'm so sorry about your sister. Why didn't you tell me?

I feel very tired.

Thanks. I type and hit send. Then I write, *But I don't have to tell anyone.*

Pulsating dots.

And his message comes whooshing in.

I know. But I thought we were friends. It feels like something you'd share.

I don't answer.

My mum pokes her head around the door, startling me. I take out my earbud. 'Are you still awake, Cleo?'

'Yeah, I am.'

'Proper awake and scrolling on your phone? Or still on the waking edge of sleep?'

'Neither?'

'Can Dad and I come in and chat?'

That's literally the last thing I want right now.

'Just for a minute?'

They're going to come in whether I like it or not.

'I guess . . .'

Mum sits next to me on my bed and Dad takes the chair from my desk.

'How was the movie?' I ask.

'Good, surprisingly. You know I'm not against a superhero remake,' Dad says while Mum crosses her eyes and shakes her head.

'It was your father's choice.'

'That tracks.' I sit up a little and shift my pillow so it's more of a back rest against the wall.

'Darling, we wanted to talk to you about something else that we did this afternoon,' Mum says. 'It might be a little difficult, but it's important to talk about it.'

Well, it's not like my day can get any worse.

'Okay . . .'

'Your grandma has expressed interest in getting a new phone,' my mum says.

I'm not sure what this has to do with me.

'Her phone's losing its battery life and she said she can't have a phone that will only last half a day, especially when she's out. Plus, she's worried she's losing her memory and wants a phone she can play games on that will help her with that.'

'Grandma's sharper than at least half of my year group at school,' I say.

'Sad for the current generation but probably true,' muses my dad.

'So why are you telling me this?' I ask.

'Well, we have a phone that's not being used right now.'

Their preamble starts to make sense. They want to give her Emmy's phone.

'We charged it and took it to the shop in the Town

Centre,' says Dad. 'And there were a lot of unread messages on it. A LOT.'

Did they see the message I sent her today? Oh my gosh, they did, no wonder they are so concerned. I have zero time to process. I want this conversation over. 'I've actually got a bit of a headache,' I say. 'Maybe we can continue this conversation later?' By later I mean never. I slide back so I'm lying down again and pull the covers over my head. It's difficult to do with Mum sitting on them. I tug at my doona harder and she gets the memo, shifts her weight so I can pull it up properly.

'Darling, we didn't open them.' Thank goodness for small mercies. I try to remember what Emmy's phone settings were. Did the messages show when they were received? They probably saw today's message. If I had any emotional bandwidth left, I'd be ridiculously embarrassed. But I just can't.

'I'm actually really tired, Mum.' My voice is muffled.

She continues anyway. 'We wanted to check in. We want you to know –'

'Need you to know,' interjects Dad.

'– That you can talk to us.'

I'm under my covers now, blinking furiously.

'I know it's not the same as talking to your sister, but we're here.'

'And if you don't want to talk to us, we can find you someone else who you'd like to talk to,' Dad says.

Mum's hand now rests on my shoulder, which is shaking ever so slightly, she rubs it gently. 'We're not upset at you, but we want you to be able to talk to someone who can respond. Sometimes you need a response.'

Mum doesn't say the words *It's time to move on*, but they are there under the surface.

'We love you, sweetie,' Dad kisses the doona covering my head and they walk out, the door clicking shut behind them.

I almost wish they had read the messages. Then I might have been forced to tell them. I would have had to tell them that after today, there is no chance of me moving on. That after today I've lost anything that it might have been possible to move on to.

Chapter Twenty-Seven

On Sunday, Mum forces me to go grocery shopping with her. I've been in bed all morning, because when I'm in bed I don't have to deal with anything else. I don't have to work out how to handle Monday. The problem is, there is no food in my bed, and Mum intercepts me on the way to the kitchen.

'Come on, Cleo, we need some things for dinner, but if you come, our first stop can be for almond croissants, plus you can pick the ice cream we get.' She has played ALL her cards early, but . . . it works.

'Mum, I'm not seven anymore,' I say. 'But just give me a minute to get out of my pjs.' Mum's 'picking the ice cream flavour' trick almost never fails. And she's used croissants to sweeten the deal. Even in my state I can't say no.

'Cookies and Cream,' I say as we grab our trolley.

'Let's wait and see what's on special.'

'Mum, if you aren't going to let me choose, why did I even come?'

She points to the half-eaten croissant that is spilling icing sugar down my chin.

Well played, Mum. She smiles at me and picks a nectarine up, smelling it before placing it back down. 'Let's get some of these,' she says. 'They smell divine.'

We make our way from the fresh fruit and vege to the refrigerated section and Mum consults her list. 'Just a few more things,' she says, then changes the topic. 'We're looking forward to Wednesday night,' Mum tells me. 'Are you feeling ready for the exhibition?'

The exhibition marks the end of the course and essentially the end of summer holidays. It's the last time I will see most of the people I met and the thought of that sets me off balance. These are people I didn't even know at the end of last year and now I'm not sure how I can live without them. But thinking back on yesterday's events, which, to be honest, I'm trying my best not to do, it's looking like a distinct possibility that I will never see them again. I give a big sigh.

'Sorry,' says Mum, noting my reaction. 'Too-hard basket?'

'It's okay, it's a fair question.' I rearrange my thoughts so I'm focusing directly on the exhibition and not everything else that feels wrapped up in it. 'I think what I'm looking forward to most about it is seeing everyone else's work. Also, it might be exciting to see what I've done up on a wall.'

'That's what I'm looking forward to. I'm excited to see what you've done.' Mum reaches to the shelf, picks up some shampoo and puts it in the trolley.

I do a double take. 'Mum, you've got the wrong one.'

'What's that?'

'Mum, put that one back, we don't need that one.'

'No?' Mum asks. 'Sometimes we get low.'

'Mum, we never get low on that one, no one uses it.'

'But I always get this one.'

'Mum.'

She stops and looks at it.

'Mum, it's for curly hair; no one has curly hair in our family anymore.'

'Oh,' says Mum, shock overwhelming her face.

'Mum, how many bottles of this do we have at home?'

'I don't know, I just put them in the cupboard so we don't run out.' Nothing frustrated Emmy more than not having the proper shampoo. 'Do you want me to look like Hagrid?' was her favourite line when I suggested using mine.

'Mum, why do you keep doing that?'

Mum holds the shampoo in her hand, but it's shaking a little. 'I'm not sure I can let go,' she says, and I don't think it's just the shampoo bottle she's talking about. 'I don't want to lose that part of my life.'

'The part that buys curly-hair shampoo?'

'The part that has a daughter who uses curly-hair shampoo.'

'Isn't it a waste, though?'

'Such a waste,' Mum says, nodding. 'Such a waste.' And I know she's not just talking about the shampoo.

Neither of us moves. Mum continues to grip the shampoo.

'Do you think you should put it back on the shelf then?' I ask. 'We probably don't need to hold onto it.' I reach out to take it from her, but her fingers grip the bottle tight.

'I didn't realise,' she says, and her hands are trembling.

'It might be time to . . .' I find myself saying, and then I stop. I don't let the next two words slip out of my mouth. Instead of saying '. . . move on', I let go of the shampoo bottle and wrap my arms around my mum.

As Mum pulls me in and holds me tight, I wonder if she hears those last two words anyway.

'I'm trying so hard,' she says and her voice catches. I feel her heartbeat against my own chest and her shaky intake of breath.

'I know, Mum,' I say as my hand makes circular movements on her back, the cotton of her t-shirt soft against my palm. 'I know you are.'

Other shoppers come by, pushing their trolleys around us, reaching past us to the shelf, and still we stand together in the aisle.

Mum and I drive back home in silence, but the words I didn't say are still tumbling round my mind.

Time to move on. Time to move on. Time to move on.

This is the first time I've reached for them, and I wonder what it means.

Chapter Twenty-Eight

On Monday morning, I really don't want to go to class. And yet, somehow, I find myself getting off the train and walking past Hyde Park towards Oxford Street. The routine of the past few weeks has sunk into me and even though the thought of turning and running is on my mind, my body follows the familiar rhythm of the walk to the Art School.

I'm not sure if this trip to class is better or worse than the first time I did it. Then, I couldn't picture what was ahead of me and it made me nervous. Now, I know what to expect and I don't want to face it. All Sunday I ignored it and this morning I've decided my best hope is to hide behind my easel. Despite this decision, my mind has been replaying Saturday's events all morning and the feelings are back. It's hard not to wish things were different. If time travel were a thing, I know what I would do.

1. I would lean away from Lachlan when he leant in to kiss me.
2. I would hold my palm in front of his mouth, a 'stop right now' moment, barring him from kissing me.
3. I wouldn't tell Mattias off.
4. I wouldn't tell Remi off.
5. I would tell Mattias about my sister.
6. I wouldn't get dumped by the wave or, if the dumping still happened, I would stay in the water with Mattias.
7. I would absolutely implore Emmy never to swerve for any animal while driving. I would tell her to hold the line. Honestly if I could time travel that would be the most important thing I would do.

Unfortunately, to my knowledge, time travel is not real, and even if it was I don't have access to it so I'm going to have to work out how to deal with my anger, disappointment and embarrassment myself somehow.

Out of all of the replays, my thoughts keep looping back to Mattias's face. I wonder if I should apologise, but then I think, *I don't have to do that.* The loop of the past events continues and I want to punch Lachlan in the face. Then my mind goes back to Mattias and I think about what might have been building and I feel angry at myself and my alarm and I really just wish my sister was alive because then I would have kissed him at Wombarra and then we would have been together and Lachlan would have realised earlier that he should just piss off and Remi and I would still be good.

When I arrive, I can see Mattias already there. He looks up but I can only bring myself to look at him out of the corner of my eye and I can't work out what he might be feeling. Probably still hurt, maybe thinking I chose Lachlan over him? Either way, I can't deal with it. I find an easel on the other side of the room and hide behind it. There is no model today; we are preparing for the exhibition.

I hear Remi as she enters the room, but I don't see her. She's saying hi to Mattias and maybe settling next to him. Part of me wants to look out and over to that side of the room. I peek out and see her legs, then I go back into hiding again.

It feels weird sitting on this side of the room, despite everything Betty has done to get us to move around. Everything is off.

By the time Betty greets us, Lachlan still hasn't shown up. Even if I don't land my punch, I know it'll be awkward when I see him; but despite my anger I miss his banter and class doesn't feel the same without him. The thought of missing him makes me uneasy and I start to wonder, did I lead Lachlan on? Was I encouraging him when he touched my arm? Did I like it when he put his arms around me? Should I have said no when he linked elbows with me? Should I have said, 'We're only friends', the way I did with Mattias? And if I said that to Mattias, why didn't I say it to Lachlan?

Maybe I did lead him on? I liked the attention he gave me, his interest, his confidence. It made me feel interesting, I didn't have to feel sad or anxious around him because he blew all those emotions away. Those were all good things, weren't they?

I step back from my artwork.

I need perspective.

I need my sister.

I need her to work it out for me. She would know what to ask me so I could figure out how I was feeling. She would know what to do. What to say. What my next steps would be. She would have made me a plan, or we would have made it together. I wouldn't need time travel because she would have prepared something actionable, something useful. But right now I have too many questions. Like why did I sideline Mattias and not Lachlan? And if there were so many things going for Lachlan, why didn't I want the kiss? Because if nothing else, that one thing is clear to me.

I didn't want to kiss Lachlan. I know that. I did NOT want to kiss Lachlan.

'This is nice,' says Betty, joining me in front of the work, her presence startling me back from my thoughts.

She leans in. 'It's an interesting choice, and the line work is good. There's an energy to this piece. I think it's almost done.' Betty moves off onto the next person, asking what pieces they are choosing and reworking for the exhibition.

The artwork I have in front of me is a sketch of Mattias's hand. I've been reworking it, playing with some pastels. Betty didn't ask why I was working on this piece. And had she asked, I'm not sure I would have answered. But this is the one question that I do know the answer to. This is the memory that returns to me when my mind is at rest. When I want to think about something positive, something that doesn't make me cry, this is where my mind goes. To this moment, drawing Mattias. My mind might float to our time walking together, it might even drift to chatting to him at Lachlan's party, but out of everything it comes back to this. So, this is the piece of art I'm working on it.

As I trace the shadows on Mattias's thumb one last time, it dawns on me.

I know why I didn't want to kiss Lachlan. It's so freaking obvious. It's because I wanted Mattias to kiss me. Despite what I told him.

It might not make sense but it's also the reason why I friend-zoned Mattias. It's because there was something there. There was something building and it scared me, because it was new and I didn't know what a relationship would look like. I didn't know how it would work and

I worried that reaching for something new would mean forgetting my sister.

I think about Mum. If she stops buying special shampoo, will that mean she forgets my sister had curly hair? Surely not. If I spend more time with Mattias, will it mean I forget the time I spent with my sister? Can't the same logic apply?

And did I lead Lachlan on? I think through the start of the day. Before we sat together in a very public place, were there any moments of intimacy?

No.

Was I insinuating that I wanted to kiss him?

No.

Did I lean forward?

No.

Did I close my eyes?

No.

Did I tell him I wanted to kiss him?

Piss off.

So, did I lead him on?

No.

Lachlan ends up coming in, super late. Just before the lunch break. Giving himself enough time to charm Betty with an apology. But he doesn't have one for me. He sits away from me and far away from Remi and Mattias, who,

I can't help but notice when people move off to lunch, is giving Lachlan the filthiest of looks. Lachlan heads out with Imogen and Amina, sharing his sunshine with them having seemingly lost interest in spending time with us after the Bondi escapade. I watch him crouching down in front of Amina while she sits on a bench during our break, casually balancing his arm next to her. Is he just going to move on like nothing happened? No acknowledgement? Captivating the next person in his sight? Am I that disposable? Who knows. What I do know is that I am furious.

Before I properly think about what I'm about to do I storm over towards them. 'Are you just going to pretend that nothing happened?' My hands are on my hips and if I were a cartoon I'd have steam coming out of my ears and nose about now.

'What do you mean?'

'I'll take that as a yes then,' I say. I'm acting entirely on impulse, and surprisingly it feels good. 'Lachlan, you're a fun guy, you have this way of making people feel important, you made me feel important and I needed that. But you can't take what's not yours. You need consent, even for a kiss. I didn't give it. I wracked my brain thinking that maybe I had led you on. But then I realised it doesn't matter. You needed to check in. If you're not getting an enthusiastic yes, then you're getting a no.'

Lachlan takes a breath as if to speak, but I hold my

finger up to silence him. 'What's worse is that you think so much of yourself that you can't believe anyone would say no to you, so you blamed it on something that happened to me. Something that you know only the smallest of details about. You need to know that is not okay. We were friends. But that's over now.'

I don't give him time to reply, it's not what he needs. Instead, I storm off. It feels amazing until I realise I don't have anywhere in particular to go. I panic for a moment, then walk into the cafe, even though I have packed my lunch, so people won't keep watching me.

I order an iced chocolate and sit down, thankful no one else is in there.

I take little sips until I notice my heart rate slowing.

Then Remi walks in. She pauses at the door, her eyes catching mine. I raise my hand, a silent hello.

She raises a hand too.

'I'm so sorry,' I mouth the words, not wanting to shout them across the room.

Remi nods and comes over to stand by my table.

I break the silence. 'I'm sorry, Remi, I really am.'

Remi doesn't reply straight away. She takes a moment to gather her thoughts. 'You know,' she says, sliding into the seat next to me, 'you telling Lachlan off is easily my favourite thing that has happened today. He needed to hear every bit of that.'

The relief I feel to have Remi back is overpowering. I feel my eyes begin to water and I blink furiously.

'Remi, I'm sorry,' I say again. 'I overreacted. I was humiliated and it was all getting too much. You have been so lovely and honestly, I'm so sorry for pushing you away.'

'That's okay, anyone would have done the same, given the circumstances.'

'I don't know if you would, Remi.'

'Who knows? I'd like to think I would have karate-chopped Lachlan.'

'You still can,' I say, and she laughs.

'Seriously though, I don't know what I would have done, maybe cried, maybe screamed. It's hard to say. But what I didn't do is message you to see how you were doing. I should have done that, but I figured you might want some space.'

'Thanks, Remi, I did.' I take a big sip of my drink. 'I think I worked a couple of things out.'

'Oh yeah?'

I hold one finger up. 'It's time for me to move on.' I hold a second finger up. 'And I do like Mattias.'

A smile sweeps across Remi's face and she nods her head as if she'd been waiting for me to voice what had become painfully obvious to her.

'So, what are you going to do?'

'I need to make a new plan.'

Chapter Twenty-Nine

I hadn't planned to tell Lachlan off, and operating in the moment felt amazing. But I think that if I'm going to sort things out with Mattias, I need something to help me.

Writing a plan without my sister is daunting. The results of the only other plan I made were not ideal, although the intent was good. Before I can write this new one, I take out the last plan I wrote. 'Plan For Making Sure Emmy Stays with Me'. I can't bring myself to crumple it or throw it out because it's been part of my journey, so I scrawl 'No longer needed' across the bottom. Then I take out my phone and, before I can think about it for too long, I delete the afternoon alarm.

I thought I would feel guilty, but the more I think about it the more I realise that this is what Emmy would have wanted, and if I'm honest with myself I know she would be more than happy for me to do this. Committing my thoughts to paper in the form of this plan is simultaneously an act of remembering my sister and an act of moving on.

Not only would my sister be happy with me, I think Jean would be impressed too.

Plan for Telling Someone You LIKE Them and Want to Be with Them

By Cleo Markson for Cleo Markson

1. *Find the person.*
2. *Tell the person.*

(Ideally don't do it in front of anyone else. Less chance of being embarrassed and chickening out or getting distracted.)

It's short and sweet and very much emblematic of my lack of experience, but surely I've captured the crux of it?

Chapter Thirty

I don't enact the plan on Tuesday morning.

We have one last life-drawing session before our exhibition on Wednesday night, but Betty does not introduce us to a new model. Instead, she hands out handheld mirrors with plastic frames.

'The final pieces of art that you will create here will be of yourself,' Betty says. 'You don't technically need the mirror, you could use your phone, and you don't have to draw your face. But there's something about looking at yourself and sharing what you see with others that is special. After all, artists have practiced like this for hundreds of years. Who are we to change the process?' She looks around the room, connecting with each of us. 'I won't set a timer, but feel free to do some quicker sketches to warm up if that has helped you in the past. Now, enjoy, and please keep your clothes on!'

There is a soft chuckle in response, then the rustle of people digging in pencil cases and the scratching sounds of marks being made on paper.

I think about what medium I'd like to use. I really enjoyed the line the ink made and I'd like to experiment with pastels some more, but something about going back to charcoal again, ending where I began, feels right. I hold the mirror in my right hand and my charcoal in my left and begin. This time, unlike the first, I don't have trouble starting.

My first sketch is quick. I look directly at the mirror and therefore my eyes stare straight at the viewer. I don't love it, and that's okay; I don't let it bother me.

I begin another. Chin pointed sidewards this time. I lightly shade in the shape of my face. Then I begin working over where my facial features sit, marking them in, checking the measurements, where they sit in relation to each other, reworking them. I stand back and assess and then, without thinking it through, use my hand to deliberately swipe across the picture, smudging it, dirtying my hand and making it look as if I am turning my head. Just like I did at the start of the course; a nod to the difficult beginning. It is messy, I think. I am messy. Life is messy. But I can't be afraid of that. I continue working, layering tighter lines on looser shades, darkening where the shadows fall on my face.

'Yes, Cleo,' says Betty as she pauses behind my work. 'Yes!' But I almost don't clock her comments as I create without trepidation, not worrying what everyone else is doing.

At the end of the session, people are smiling and swapping artworks. I decide to keep my best one for my mum. I'll frame it for her birthday. I consider giving one to Mattias but the timing's not right and it feels weaker to shove a picture at him hoping it will solve everything.

No, stick with the plan, I tell myself. If not today, then tomorrow.

Chapter Thirty-One

The last day of the course feels like a crazy attempt to put a lid on an overflowing jar of steam. Why steam would be in a jar, I don't know. But these experiences we've had can't be contained to this week, it feels like they will continue to stretch out, to affect our lives in different ways forever.

We bustle about finalising our artist statements and giving them to Betty for her to hang. We gather with the printmakers and ceramicists again and Rachael Ramirez gives us a wrap-up speech and provides instructions for the evening's exhibition. We reflect on our week and fill in feedback surveys where it feels impossible to express what we have learnt and how we have grown. Then we pack up the room that has become our home over these last four weeks. I don't know how I feel, but I'm focusing on each task as it comes and trying not to think about the fact that everything is ending.

The girls take turns in the bathroom stalls; jeans and tees are swapped for dresses or loose tailored pants and cute camis. Layered necklaces and winged eyeliner are added as we crowd around the mirrors, gushing over each other and the weeks that have been. We kill time before the exhibition starts by taking a walk together as a big group and somehow end up at Macca's because that's where we fit. We sprawl out, taking over the joint, conversations loud, energy high. Each moment merges into the next and time feels like it has been sped up, this day existing as a montage of moments, until we return one last time.

Our parents and supporters have been told to meet us outside the exhibition space, and when they start showing up we split off from our friends and huddle in smaller clumps. There is the awkward push and pull of not knowing whether to stay with them, introduce them to our friends, or to slip away and spend the remaining time with the people we have come to know.

Throughout it all, I am aware of where Mattias is. Aware of my plan that I have not yet put in place. Painfully aware that my time is running out.

When the doors to the exhibition open, it feels a little like magic. There are fairy lights hung inside and champagne flutes with sparkling apple juice, appropriate for the mostly underage crowd.

I wasn't sure where my body of work would be hung.

When I see it, my breath catches. I feel a sense of pride welling up, along with the prickle of a tear, which I quickly wipe away. My work is not as detailed as Mattias's, or as technical as Remi's, yet it's mine and it displays what I've learnt and how far I've come. It represents what I want. Natasha Shandinni's artworks were titled with things women give up, but each of my titles shares what I desire. The one of Nerida that my mum liked is tilted *Freedom*. I've called the one of Miia *Poise*. There is one of Jesse titled *Confidence*. The last one is simply called *You*.

After making my own way around the room, I find my parents and step between them, draping my arms around them both. 'Mum and Dad, thank you so much for coming,' I say.

'We are just so proud of you,' Mum says, her hand reaching up to mine and squeezing it tight.

'Thank you for making me attend. I know I wouldn't have come had it not been for your –' I pause as I look for the right word '– encouragement. And I just really appreciate it. Thank you.'

Mum loosens her hand from mine and turns to face me, wrapping me in a hug. Then she steps back and puts her hands on my shoulders. 'We love you, sweetie, and even if we did have to *encourage*' – she uses her fingers to form air quotes when she says the word – 'you did all this on your own. Well done.'

'Thanks, Mum. Um, if you don't mind, I've got a couple more things I need to do so just go when you are ready and I'll make my own way home if you've left.'

Mum looks quizzical but nods.

People stand in small groups. Some students show their parents around, some stand with friends. People who were unknown to each other at the start of course have forged strong bonds. I'm reminded of the opening speech from my first day. Rachael Ramirez was right, connections have been made.

I take a step back from the group. I can do this. This summer has brought so many firsts already and this is going to be another of them. Mattias is talking to Amina and Remi. I make a beeline towards them and launch right in before realising that I haven't planned exactly what I am going to say. 'Mattias, before you go, I have something to show you.' It is a stupid thing to say; I have nothing to show him.

'Sure,' he says. 'I can come now if you want?'

'Yep,' I say before my nerves get the best of me.

Mattias motions with his hand as if to say lead the way and I walk towards the chapel door then turn left and walk away from the lights and noise. When it feels like we are alone, I stop.

'What is it?' Mattias asks, pausing next to me and looking around.

I turn to face him, chin raised, and search his eyes with my own. It's now or never. 'I don't have anything to show you. And I still didn't bring you back your shirt.'

'No?'

'No.'

His eyebrows raise ever so slightly at my answer. 'Are you going to keep it forever?'

'Maybe. I'm not sure, that wasn't what I wanted to talk to you about.'

'No?'

'No! Stop derailing me.'

'Okay . . .'

'I didn't tell you about my sister. But I didn't tell him either, not properly, it was an offhand comment. But he doesn't know anything.'

'Hang on, can I stop you there? Just for a second?'

'Why?'

'I need to apologise. I'm sorry. I shouldn't have messaged you. That was about me, not you. I was jealous. I know we're friends, but I kept thinking maybe there was something more. But either way, it doesn't matter, because you're right. You don't have to tell anyone. I just hope I haven't blown my chances. And if you want to talk, then I guess you know where I live.'

His apology melts away any apprehension I have. 'I do want to talk to you, but you keep interrupting,' I say, but he can see I'm smiling. 'You know, I'm going to miss all of this.'

'Me too.'

Come on, Cleo, just say it.

'I'm going to miss you.'

The distance between us shortens. Mattias holds my gaze and my heart squeezes.

'I didn't tell you about my sister. Like you said, it is up to me when I want to tell people, but I did *want* to tell you.'

His eyes met mine again and I feel comfortable continuing. 'I know I had so many opportunities to tell you, and I do wish I had taken one of them.' I take a big breath. 'At the start of my sister Emmaline's last year of school she was in a car accident. She swerved to miss something, some sort of animal probably, we don't know what, and lost control of the car. One day she was there and the next? Gone. But I couldn't let her go.' I pause, take another breath, then continue. 'When we were sitting at the pool, my phone didn't ring. It was my alarm. I've not told anyone this before, but I had it set to go off at four pm. And every day at four pm when it sounded, I took a moment and thought about my sister. It helped me feel close to her, helped me feel like I won't forget her.' I take yet another big breath. 'But when we were sitting together and it went off, I was so startled. I was so caught up in being with you that I didn't even realise it was my alarm. And it freaked me out. I felt like I was losing her all over again.'

I let in sink in.

'I wish you'd told me,' says Mattias.

'I mean, a normal person would, but does a normal person set an alarm at the same time every day to file through their memories of their sister?' The question has set him up to fail. 'Actually, don't answer that.' I swallow and gather my thoughts. 'I think I was holding onto the past so tightly that when I tried to reach for something new, I couldn't grip onto it, I couldn't gain purchase. I was so busy clutching at my memories of what life used to be like, desperately trying not to lose it, that the good stuff that came my way kept slipping through my fingers. I think I might have misled you earlier and I didn't mean to.'

Mattias steps back, and I realise I'm making a mess of it. *Step two of the plan, Cleo,* I remind myself. *Tell the person.*

'Sorry, bad choice of words.' I instinctively grab his arm and pull him so that he is now standing next to me, our backs against the wall. I let my hand drop but I don't move away, and my hand now rests against his arm. It'll be easier to say if I don't look at him. 'I said we should be friends, but I didn't mean it.' I'm looking straight ahead, not at him.

'What did you mean?'

'I mean I'm worried *you* will slip through my fingers. I don't want friendship. Well, I do but not *just* that. I want more.'

'More?' Mattias says, and even though I'm not looking at him I can hear the smile on his lips.

I turn to face him, my hand still on his arm. He turns towards me, meeting my gaze. The distance between us has closed so much it's like we have begun to occupy the same space.

I feel a small frown form on my forehead, and I am biting my lip. 'I want more.'

'Cleo?' asks Mattias.

'Yes?'

'Your works in the exhibition, the one of the hand, the one titled *You* . . . Is that my hand, is that me?'

He lifts his arm and brings his hand gently to my face. He smooths my forehead with his thumb, then brings it to my lips. He traces a line along my lips then rests his hand under my chin, raising it slightly.

'Do *you* want more?' I ask.

I look at his beautiful face. And he's not answering, but in this moment? In this moment, I don't mind. His eyes flick down to my lips and back up to my eyes again and his thumb traces tiny circles on my jawbone. I am leaning forward, leaning closer to him, my mind willing him to do the same. And then as if he is mirroring me, he leans in too and our heads are close now and I can see his eyelashes dark and long and I wish for a split second that mine looked more like that but only for a second because I feel like I am drinking him in.

In answer to my question, Mattias leans the tiniest bit forward. Then I close the distance between us and his lips brush gently against mine. He pulls back, ever so slightly, assessing my expression. 'Yes,' he says. 'I hope this is what you meant by more.' And I feel like my heart will explode.

I wrap my arms around his neck, and he spins me so my back is now against the wall.

'Yes,' I say. 'Absolutely yes!', and he kisses me again. This time it's longer and deeper and his body is pressed against mine and I never want the moment to end.

When we finally break apart, he rests his forehead against mine. 'This is what I've wanted for a long time,' he says.

'How long?'

'Since you came in late on the first morning of art school.'

'I thought you didn't even know I was sitting next to you?'

'When I saw you at back of the room looking adorably flustered, I shuffled over so there was a spot next to me, hoping you might come and sit there.'

Wait, what? 'You saw me then?'

Mattias leans back, seeing my surprise. 'I was so pleased when you sat in that space.'

'I think you might need to reassess your definition of space.'

'There really wasn't enough room, was there?'

'No,' I agree, smiling at the memory. Then I frown. 'If you noticed me then, why didn't you talk to me, introduce yourself?'

'I didn't know what to say, and we were so squashed. I thought it was easier to talk to you outside. I panicked.'

'I just thought you were being super rude.'

'It's the impression I sometimes give. I'm sorry. I went to find you outside, but you were talking to Lachlan and . . .' Mattias trails off.

'There was history with him,' I fill in.

'That's right. And maybe my frustration at him filtered down on you.'

'So that drink you spilled on me at the party was on purpose?'

'No, of course not.'

I think back to that night, the party feeling so long ago.

'You know, I liked that night,' he says.

'Go on.'

'It was the first time we talked properly. And you saw me, not just as an outsider but as someone people want to be around. It was so surprising. I couldn't believe you saw me as being the exact opposite of what everyone at school sees.'

'What is wrong with them?' I ask.

Mattias laughs and continues. 'I feel like I saw you that day too. I liked that you pushed me to talk with you. Challenged me. It felt like you knew what you wanted. There was a confidence there.'

I almost laugh. 'You know, I feel so unsure about life all the time,' I say. 'I honestly have no idea about this confidence you speak of!'

'No, it's there. It has to be. You are worried about things and yet you do them anyway. You push yourself beyond where you feel comfortable, and you take others along for the ride.'

'Are you sure you're not confusing me with Remi?' I ask.

'No.' He shakes his head. 'Did Remi seem worried or nervous about coming here?'

'No.'

'Did you feel nervous and worried about coming?'

'Yes.'

'And yet you did it anyway. Were you worried about coming down to my place the other week?'

'Oh my gosh, did you see the sweat stains?'

'No; I got the impression that driving down wasn't straight forward, but you did it. You impress me and worry me and even though I know you are brave and strong, I want to be there for you, when or if you need me.'

I draw him back to me and kiss him again.

Plan for your Final Year of School

By Emmaline Markson, for Cleo Markson, **updated by Cleo**
~~I've started year 12 and here's what I've learnt so far. You won't need this plan right away, but I hope it will help when you get there.~~

1. *Choose subjects you like, bonus points if you are good at them.* **Fingers crossed, I've done this**
2. *Listen in class. This feels a little obvious, but you'd be surprised at the number of classmates I've seen disappointed with their results when they've literally paid no attention all semester.* ✓
3. *Study. It's a boring one, but important. ~~Depending on where I end up, I'll help if I can, except for art, obviously. Unless you want suggestions on the best ways to draw stick figures and worms. I reckon I'm pretty good at both!~~* **Will need to get started**

4. *Keep your life in balance. I've made comments about the school stuff, but you have to balance it out with everything else. So, with that in mind:*
   a) *Continue swimming.* ***Doing***
   b) *Get a job and start saving.* ***Doing***
   c) *Start to build your social life!!!* ✓
5. *To help with 4c: find your friends. Your real ones.* ✓
6. *In your free time, try some new things. My suggestions are as follows:*
   - *Explore Sydney some more.* ✓
   - *Go to a party, if you haven't done that already. (I know it's not your usual scene, but it's a rite of passage – and remember 4c!)* ✓
   - *First kiss?!* ~~*Who knows, maybe by the time you hit year 12 this will already have already happened? (I hope so, but if not, here is my quick pep talk . . . You said you can't comprehend anyone liking you enough to stick their tongue down your throat – your words, not mine – but maybe you need to be ready? Despite what you think, you ARE very likeable!! And so is kissing. For more details see my very useful 'Plans for First Kisses'.)*~~ ✓ **– my second kiss was very likeable**
7. *Work out what you want* ~~*to do when you finish year 12*~~ ✓ **(It's Mattias, and it's okay to work out the other stuff as I go)**

You got this, Cleo! It's going to be great. **I think it might be!**

Acknowledgements

First of all, thank you so much to the team at Penguin Random House. This book exists because of all of you and I am very grateful. Thank you to Lisa Riley, my publisher. Thank you for saying yes to *Drawing Nudes*. What a dream come true!

To Suzanne O'Sullivan, thank you so very much for seeing *Drawing Nudes* and understanding what I was trying to do with it and knowing how to make it so much better. I have loved the process of editing this book with you. Claire de Medici, thank you for your eagle eyes and for your help fine-tuning this book.

Thank you to my publicist Maddy Taplin and marketer Jess Pearson, and thank you to Hazel Lam for the beautiful cover. It is a work of art in and of itself. And speaking of the cover, thank you to Melina Marchetta for being such an inspiration and for the wonderful blurb. I could not have even dreamt of having your name on my book. Thank you times a million.

Thank you to Laura Harris for listening to me pitch this book at the SCBWI Professional Development Day at the State Library of NSW, for responding with such joy and belief in this project and for representing me and my book. Your genuine care for me and *Drawing Nudes* made the journey towards publication so much smoother and more enjoyable. I'm very thankful that we got to work together.

Thank you to SCBWI Australia East for the opportunities you provide to authors and illustrators. You do so much work and it doesn't go unnoticed or unappreciated. Thank you for seeing merit in my pitch and giving me the platform to share it. Thank you also to my SCBWI Retreat Group 2023.

To my KidLit West buddies, Artelle, Michelle, Dannielle, Abbey and Sharara, I appreciate you so much. Thank you for your feedback, encouragement and support.

Thank you to my online critique group who saw early drafts of different scenes. Shae, Anita and Raema, you kept me going.

Thank you to my twin sister Aimee and my mother Ruth for reading an early version of this book. Your love and enthusiasm encouraged me on. (Also if I can't write a book my sister and mum love, then what does that even say?) Thank you to Mum and Dad for building a family that loves words and stories even if it did mean sacrificing conversation for reading time at the dinner table.

Kiah Thomas, remember that time you told me I should write something longer? My brilliant friend, I could not have done this without you. I would not have done it without you. I love how invested you were in Cleo's story and how you always knew how to make it better. And even when I didn't want to listen, you were always right. Thank you.

Finally, a big thank you to my husband Paul and to Ollie, Elena and Lucy. Thank you for your support, for putting up with me, and for keeping me humble. Love you all.

About the Author

As a year 11 student, Zoe Gaetjens attended a life drawing workshop where she failed to plan anything significant. She has since traded her charcoal for a laptop and writes books for children and young adults. When Zoe is not writing she works as a high school English teacher. She believes that the books you love as a teenager stay with you forever. Zoe lives just outside of Sydney with her husband and three kids.